Model (mis)Behaviour

MODEL ACT

duet

First Edition.

ISBN: 978-1-8383638-7-1

Cover design: © The Pretty Little Design Co.

Editor: SB Proofreading

Model (mis)Behaviour

MODEL ACT duet

K. LOWRIE

To second chances,

One

Atticus

'AH, FUDGE BISCUITS!'

I looked at my thumb and winced. Somehow, it had already turned red, and I swore I could actually see it throbbing. Served me right for trying to lift these heavy boxes all by myself, although, I wasn't sure who *would* have been able to help me. Scarlet could have if she was home, but the girl would blow over in the wind, so there was no way she could handle these boxes filled with books.

Scar had been begging me for months—or a lot longer—to leave halls and move in with her, but I'd always pushed the idea aside. It wasn't that I didn't want to live with my best friend, not at all. It was because I'd wanted to finish university on my own merit, with no help from anyone.

Stupid, I know, but that was the way my mind worked.

I'd been adamant that I could graduate, and then get a place for myself, *or* move in here with Scar, but as somebody who paid half the rent. Right now, she'd be lucky if I had enough money to pay for half of the weekly food shopping. Being a broke student wasn't what it was cracked up to be—not that anybody had told me it would be easy—but last week had been the final straw.

As the oldest person in my halls, I'd found the constant partying a bit of an issue. The odd Friday or Saturday night, yeah, fair play, but when the noise and uninvited guests happened *every, single, night* then I knew I couldn't hack it much longer. Plus, somebody in the night had come into my room and peed in my wastepaper bin thinking it was a toilet. Disgusting.

So, not long after that incident, I rang Scarlet in frustrated tears about my situation and she opened up her apartment to me with open arms, free of charge. Of course, I intended to pay her back for every penny once I graduated and got a great job.

Over the past two days, I'd been moving in not only my things from halls but the things that had been at my parents' house still that I hadn't had the room for, like my bookcases and vast collection of books. Being a twenty-seven-year-old who still hadn't got her shit together didn't feel great. I could tell you that for free.

Sucking my thumb to ease the sting, I surveyed the room. Boxes were piled high in the right-hand corner, and you couldn't see the floor through all the books I'd just dropped.

'Eurgh,' I groaned, talking to myself, a habit of mine. 'Great job, Atticus.'

My name had caused some issues growing up. I had lived near the city, and honestly, a lot of kids I'd attended school with had, shall we say, unique names? You know, like Chardonnay or Beryl, or something equally exciting. I'd tried to tell everybody that Atticus Finch was one of the greatest characters in literature, and that I was honoured to have the name. (Well, maybe I wasn't quite so honoured the year *Go Set A Watchman* came out, but I did my best to ignore that as canon).

"But Atticus is a boy's name!" The other kids had said, and honestly, by the time I reached sixteen I would just answer, "Yep, I'm aware." Once you stopped putting up with people's shit, they usually started to leave you alone.

A shrill, ringing tone echoed throughout the room, and I just knew that it was a call from Scarlet, wondering if she needed to send round a paramedic. The girl knew I was clumsy, and that I usually managed to hurt myself while standing still. *She wasn't wrong.*

'Oh, crap, where did I put you?' I asked the air, hoping that my phone would somehow gain the capability to speak and answer me. Sadly, it did not.

I walked around the boxes, trying my best to avoid the books and papers that littered the floor, using the ringtone as a beacon.

'Gotcha!' I said triumphantly, finding my phone on top of the pile of the boxes in the corner. 'Hello,' I answered, not even bothering to look at the caller ID first, and put it on loud-speaker so I could continue doing whatever it was I was attempting to do.

'How's it going?' Scarlet's voice came through the speaker, bright and cheery, but also slightly sceptical. 'All limbs still attached?'

'Ha, funny. I'll have you know I am completely unharmed,' I responded in what I believed was a breezy tone. She saw through it instantly.

'You've hurt yourself, then,' she said, chuckling. 'What did you do this time?'

'Dropped a box and somehow trapped my thumb. No biggie, though.'

'Yeah, sure.' She muttered something to somebody, then said, 'Look, I've got to go, but I was just calling to ask if you wanted to come to the wrap party with me tonight.'

Scarlet was an aspiring actress—a lot of emphasis on the word *aspiring*—but recently she'd been playing a small part in the background of a big blockbuster movie. She hadn't been allowed to tell me much about it, but I knew how excited she was.

'So, what do you say?' she asked when I didn't instantly answer her.

'Errrr,' I said, not really wanting to say yes, but knowing that she would twist my arm eventually so it would probably be easier to just agree. 'Sure.'

'Yay!' she squealed. 'Get yourself dolled up baby g and I'll be home in two. Love you!'

'Love you!' I replied. The beep of her hanging up came, and I sighed and slumped to the ground. A wrap party for a big film? That meant that there would be *famous* people there, and I definitely didn't have an outfit suitable for that kind of event. I barely had enough leggings to lounge around in, let alone a killer dress and heels that would impress people of note.

Somehow, in the three years that Scar had been trying to break into the business, I'd managed to avoid attending any of her soirees. Most of the time I was too busy studying, or had just outright told her no. I wasn't a partygoer, as a rule, and I felt uncomfortable in those kinds of situations. Being clumsy, I usually ended up flat on my arse, either slipping in spilled drinks, or nearly breaking an ankle trying to walk in heels on the sticky carpet.

'Guess I better get a move on,' I huffed to myself as I picked up a book from the floor. Scar said she'd be home in two hours, which meant I needed to get sorted, and fast.

I made a quick to-do list in my head: Tidy the room, find an outfit, shower and wash my hair, then get glammed up.

Fun, fun, fun.

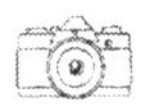

Two hours later, I was still standing in the exact same position, in the middle of my new bedroom, staring at the surrounding mess.

My bedroom looked like a tornado had hit it, clothes and shoes all over the room with no rhyme or reason. Somehow, a bra had managed to attach itself to my ceiling fan and was hanging there limply.

'Atti!' Scar called through the apartment, making her way towards me, and then appearing in my doorway. 'Oh, wow. You've made great progress.'

'No need to be sarcastic,' I replied, out of breath.

'Why do you sound like you just ran a marathon?' she asked, raising a perfectly sculpted eyebrow at me. Scar always looked glamorous, and always had done, even before she started to pursue an acting career.

'I've been running around this room like a headless chicken for the last hour trying to find something to wear tonight. Believe me, there is nothing suitable in any of these boxes.'

'I'm sure you have something,' she said, rifling through the clothes I'd laid out on my bed. 'Have you still got that one shoulder, green satin number?'

'I think so,' I replied, 'but I'm not sure if it fits anymore.' I'd gained a bit of weight since starting my degree, mostly through stress eating during exam times. Also, the kitchen at halls had been *vile*. Nobody cleaned up after themselves, and it had got to the point where I kept my own cutlery in my room in order to keep it safe—and sanitary.

'I'm sure it does,' she said, her head in one of the many boxes. She reappeared, and in went her hand to snatch out the dress in question. She pulled it out triumphantly. 'I've got you now!'

Her shoulder-length blonde curls bounced with the movement, and it hit me for maybe the thousandth time, that she was the beautiful blonde that a lot of people aspired to be. She had an effortlessly chic style, and her smile drew you in. The girl was friendly to everybody and always managed to make friends in any situation. I'd never been that lucky, always being the one to stand alone, silently surveying the room.

'You will look perfect in this, with your dark hair up and a bold red lip,' she said, her white teeth beaming at me. All I could do was stare at her, wondering what had put so much pep in her step.

'You okay?' I asked, raising my eyebrows at her. 'Any reason you're so excited for tonight?'

'No reason,' she said, closing her mouth afterwards—a move that I knew well. It meant she was hiding something from me, or that she wanted to tell me what it was but wasn't able to for some reason or another.

'Spill,' I demanded, not letting her worm her way out of it.

'I can't,' she whined, making a zipping motion with her hand across her lips. I rolled my eyes at her theatrics.

'How old are we? Five?' I crossed my arms in front of my chest and tapped my toe, waiting for her response.

'Atticus, don't take this the wrong way, but man, you look like your mother right now.'

'You cheeky cow!' I leapt forward to grab her and tickle her sides. Her laugh was loud in my ear, but I wasn't going to relent. This meant war.

'No!' she called, as the two of us crashed onto the clothes covering the bed.

'Take it back,' I told her, easing up on her slightly, but not moving my hands just in case she doubled down and made it worse.

'I take it back,' she said with a chuckle and I moved away from her and sat up, my legs over the edge of the bed.

'So, what *you* gonna wear?' I asked her, wondering what one of her many, *many* outfits she planned to wow everybody with.

'Not sure yet. Come to my room and help me decide?'

'Only if you help me with my face.' I'd never had much skill at make-up, and Scar had always followed every trend and knew all the latest fashions, so I usually let her work her magic on me when we went out on the town—even though Scar herself chose to dress like a 1950s vixen and never actually used her knowledge of the latest trends for her own gain.

'Duh,' she said, poking me in the ribs. 'Come on, then.'

'Give me a sec, I just want to find some underwear that can go under this dress.'

'Okay, I'll go make a head start.'

Scar left my room, and once I knew she was out of my

eyeline, I flopped back down onto the bed, and looked up at the ceiling. For some unknown reason, the ceiling was textured like an old-fashioned popcorn ceiling, but smoother, and the way the light hit it caused different patterns to form.

I'd only moved in two days ago, but I'd already stared up at this ceiling for too long, transfixed by the different patterns. Also, my eyes played tricks after a while and the raised parts looked like they were inverted instead. *The excitement, I know*.

Realistically, I should have said no to going out tonight. I wasn't in the mood at all, and I really didn't want to be that dumpy girl in the corner while Scarlet was being her social-butterfly self, charming everybody in the room.

'Hey, Scar!' I called out. Her bedroom was separated from mine by a large bathroom, so we could communicate via speech while in bed if we wanted to. Although usually we messaged, even though we were under the same roof.

'Yeah,' she called back, and I could hear her opening closet doors—her search for an outfit was well underway. The girl owned too many clothes, and barely wore them more than once, just in case she was spotted or papped. She rarely had been, though.

'Is it a free bar?' I asked, the idea having just come to my mind.

'Yeah, of course it is! Why else would I be so excited?'

'Well, this changes things,' I said to myself, rubbing my hands together with glee like some second-rate movie villain. I snorted with a laugh. What a dork.

'Huh?' Scar called, and I laughed louder.

'Just talking to myself,' I said. She made a noise in

response, and I smiled. We'd been friends for long enough now that Scar was aware of my little quirks.

I'd always found it hard being her best friend. Scarlet was so easy-going and out there; the friendly one. Then there was me, the awkward, clumsy, shy one who had struggled to make friends. The two of us had been inseparable ever since, aged five, on World Book Day, we'd both come to school dressed as our favourite princesses and that shit connected you. She'd always been the girl the guys wanted, the girl that got invited on dates every weekend, and was never short of secret admirers on Valentine's Day.

When we'd turned fifteen, a boy had asked me on a date and I totally believed that it was a joke. That his mates must have set him up to it as a dare of sorts. It took him over a year to convince me to give him a real chance. It had been charming and endearing...and fake. I shook my head, trying to banish those dark thoughts. Not a great path to head down, that was for sure. Especially, as I didn't feel confident about this evening as it was.

There were times when I let the thought of him enter my mind, and I classed those as my weak moments. I needed to have less of them.

Begrudgingly, I got up and headed slowly to Scar's room, dragging my feet behind me with every step.

'Come on, hoe,' she called, obviously sensing that I was taking my time about getting ready.

'Yeah, yeah,' I replied with a deep sigh. Standing in the doorway of her room, I saw her still standing in front of the open closet doors, the noise of screeching hangers across the rail in my ear as she looked at her options. 'Do I *have* to come with you?'

'Yes! We haven't been out together in *forever,* and I want us to have a night of letting our hair down. You've been working so hard on your degree, and I feel like we've barely spent time together.'

'Scar, I just moved in to live with you. We're going to be sick of each other soon enough.'

'I could never get sick of you. Sick of your lack of cleanliness, however? Potentially.' We both laughed at her words.

'Fine, but I want all the drinks *and* you have to get me cheesy chips once we leave,' I told her, meaning it. Cheesy chips were a drunk must.

'Deal.'

Two

Parker

'PARKER, could you move slightly to the right, please?'

Bruce, the photographer, called out to me, and I adjusted my position accordingly. I'd been on enough shoots now to know the drill. I could take any direction and perfect it. *What can I say?* It was one of my superpowers.

'Perfect. Now don't move a muscle,' he said. The shutter clicked, and the lights flashed with every image he took.

Staying as still as I possibly could, my mind wandered back to my very first modelling shoot, back when I had just turned eighteen. It had been an underwear shoot, and I had been prepping for weeks in the gym, trying to get into the best shape I could. I'd been overly cocky, telling everybody who would listen that I would be the next best thing, and that my Calvin Klein covered junk would be on every billboard in the city.

I'd been very wrong.

None of the photos ever saw much more than a social-feed grid, and I still hadn't lived down the embarrassment with the lads. Every time we all got together, they blasted me with jokes and banter. I could shrug it off, easy. Really, they had a valid point. I'd tried too hard to use poses I didn't understand, and I definitely didn't know at that point how to find my light.

Lucky for me, it was all different now.

'Turn, slightly. That's it!'

I'd been to university, to study something I now didn't use, but during that time I had picked up more shoots, and had slowly built a name for myself in the industry. From an early age, I'd always enjoyed being in front of a camera, or a mirror, and my mum constantly told anybody that would listen that she knew that I couldn't be so handsome for no reason. Jane Daniels was one of my biggest supporters these days, sharing every shoot on her face-ache page for all the other desperate face-wives. Bless.

After another hour's worth of instructions, Bruce called the shoot to a halt.

'Lunch break,' he called, stepping away from behind his camera for the first time all day. 'Claire, make sure that Parker gets a touch up, please. Then call Alexa Cummings and confirm the warehouse shoot for three weeks' time.'

Claire, the photographer's assistant, handed me a dressing gown to cover myself with during the break. Not that I was uncomfortable in only underwear, but it definitely made other people uncomfortable at times.

'Thank you,' I said, and then decided to turn on the charm. She was quite cute, even if her outfit showed how underpaid she was in her role. 'You look amazing today, Claire. You have a beautiful smile.'

'Th-thanks, Mr Daniels.' She blushed, and I watched as it spread like a rash to her entire face. I smiled widely at her, showing off my pearly whites. I'd been told my smile could blind, and I used that to my advantage 99.9% of the time. 'The lunch table is over there, sir.'

I nodded my thanks and gravitated towards the spread that had been prepared. Platters of sandwiches and the likes were causing the table to groan on its legs. I grabbed a plate and made my way down the line, taking a bit of everything.

Heading to a seat in the corner, my phone began to ring from the pocket of the gown. *Good old Claire.* She deserved a raise. Maybe I'd mention it to Brucey boy when we were done.

'Y'ello,' I answered, knowing who would be on the other end without looking at the screen.

'Yo, what's up?' Jackson asked, speaking loudly to be heard over the murmurs in the background.

'Lunch,' I replied, not needing to say any more than that.

He groaned, and said, 'I would kill for some lunch right now. Dennis is really busting some balls.'

'Tough day?'

'The toughest, but there *is* a silver lining. Tonight's the wrap party. You in?'

Jackson James was the best—and if you listened to the ladies (or my mum)—the hottest actor around at the moment. He'd started acting at age five and had somehow managed to get through the curse of the child star. It helped that he had a stable head on his shoulders now. He hadn't always, but a couple of years ago, he really turned his life around.

He'd been shooting a big film for the last three months, and I knew he was proud of his performance. Wouldn't be shocked if come February there was awards buzz about him.

'Sure, dude. Any hot girls on set?' I asked, knowing that film sets were usually a hotbed for hot women who wanted a piece of the action. I wasn't as famous, or as well known, as Jackson, but I did alright for myself. The paparazzi recently had been cropping up wherever Jackson and I went on our nights out, and it gave me a slight buzz.

'There's this one girl, but she's off limits.' He chuckled, and I knew he had plans to tap that.

'Ah, it's like that is it?' I waggled my eyebrows, even though he couldn't see me.

'We'll see. So, you game?' he asked.

'Of course. I'll be back at the flat by five. Surely they don't need me to stand around in my tighty whities for much longer.' The two of us had been roommates for the last five years. We'd met after I'd left university, and had moved into a house share where he happened to be living, too. Since then, both of us had earned enough money to move out into a flat—just us two. We could have got our own bachelor pads, but for some reason unknown to me, Jackson didn't like being alone.

'Sounds like such a struggle for you, and dude, never refer to them as tighty whities again.'

I laughed at his reaction, enjoying any time that I managed to get a rise out of him. Jackson always tried to act cool as a cucumber, and I'd made it a part of my life's purpose to ruffle his feathers whenever the opportunity presented itself.

'You love it,' I teased. 'Right, dickhead. I need to eat before Bruce starts barking orders again.'

'Yeah, yeah,' he said. 'See you tonight.'

'Later, dude.'

We hung up, and I ate the food on my plate. A wrap party sounded like just the thing to get me out of my funk. These last few months, I'd barely dated anybody, and when I said the word "dated" I meant fucked. I'd been too busy jetting around for shoots and shows that I hadn't had the time to find a booty call that didn't want anything serious.

'Are you ready for a touch up, Mr Daniels?' A girl asked me, timid and clearly uncomfortable about having interrupted my private time.

'I think I am,' I glanced at her name tag, so placed that I *had* to glance at her ample chest in the process. Laurel. Interesting name.

She giggled, and the sound went straight to my dick. *Down, boy.*

'Right this way,' she said, gesturing for me to follow her. I obeyed, and instead of directing me to one of the make-up chairs in the far corner, she walked us into a corridor where the private offices were.

I would enjoy this.

WALKING INTO THE APARTMENT, I waited for the pitter-patter of paws on the hardwood floor. Within moments, a large mass of hair bounded towards me, his tongue hanging out—over-excited to see me.

'Hey, boy,' I said, scratching underneath Radley's chin. Radley was my two-year-old brown Newfoundland, and even though he was still a baby in my eyes, he definitely wasn't the size of one. He was just about fully grown, and he was a lump. 'How has Auntie Cassie been treating you?'

'Cassie has been treating him fine, as always.' My sister came into view and rolled her eyes at me, her ponytail bouncing as she looked around me, clearly hoping that I'd be arriving home with Jackson. She had a crush on him, and if she wasn't nearly ten years younger than us, I'd be worried, but I knew Jackson and he wouldn't go there.

'He's not with me, Cass.' Radley stood up on his hind legs, pawing at my chest, trying to give me a slobbery kiss that I wouldn't allow. At six foot one, I should be a lot taller than my own dog, but standing like this, Radley reached my shoulders. I got him when I saw the advertisement for a local shelter that had been given a litter of 'Newfies', and they were struggling to find the last one a home. The moment I visited him, we'd connected, and I researched all that I could about the breed. It also helped Jackson when I travelled for work, so he was never alone in the flat.

'Bummer,' she replied, popping her chewing gum. Cassie was my youngest sister, and she'd only just turned eighteen. She hadn't gone to university, and while she was trying to figure out what to do with her life, I'd asked her to dog-sit Radley on the days I wouldn't be home for him. He was a beast of a dog, and he couldn't be left alone for long. 'Need me to stick around?'

'Not today,' I told her, as I knew she didn't want to 'stick around' to spend time with her big bro. I made my way into our large open-plan kitchen, and both Cassie and Radley followed me.

'You're no fun,' she whined, grabbing her mobile off of the counter and looking at the screen, already bored by me.

'Got plans tonight?' I asked her, even though I'd already anticipated her answer. Since turning eighteen a few months ago, every weekend she and her friends have been out in the city, crawling from pub to bar until they couldn't stand anymore. My parents were so proud.

'There's a big event happening at Muse, so I think me and the girls are gonna try and score an in.'

'Hate to break it to you, little sis, but that's where I'll be tonight and I doubt you want to see your bro in action.' We'd made a rule when she became of legal drinking age that we wouldn't go to the same places at the same time. I worried that anybody I was with would try to hook up with her, and *she* worried that her friends would try to hook up with *me*.

'*In action*?' she asked, raising her eyebrows with a look of disgust on her face. 'You're making it sound like you're gonna be a stripper, or something.'

'Definitely not,' I told her with a laugh. 'Tonight's the wrap party for Jackson's new film.'

The moment the words had left my lips, I wanted to cram them back in. Cassie's whole face changed, and she let out a high-pitched squeal. *Shit*.

'Jackson will be with you at Muse? I have to tell Amanda!' Her fingers started flying across her phone, obviously messaging her friends about the news I'd let slip.

'Do not show up!' I warned her, trying to convey my seriousness. 'I won't vouch for you to get you past the bouncers.'

'Yeah, yeah,' she said, not listening to a word. 'Love you, bro. Gotta dash!'

I watched as she flew through the kitchen and living area, grabbed her things, and rushed out of the front door.

Honestly, I was so lucky that my other sister, Zara, was a little more level-headed. She'd never given me a stress headache, and she definitely at no point had tried to hook up with any of my friends. Probably had something to do with the fact that she'd had a serious girlfriend since she was sixteen, but still.

Within ten minutes, Jackson arrived home to find me laying on the sofa staring up at the ceiling. I'd poured myself a large tumbler of whiskey and was trying to relax before the night to come.

'You alright?' he asked, his tone worried.

'Yeah, just trying to get rid of a stress headache, the norm.'

'Cassie just leave?' he asked, and I nodded. I had never asked him, so I wasn't certain, but I had a feeling that he purposely made sure that he came home after she'd left. He'd always been nice to her, but he knew of her crush, and he didn't want to fan those flames. Good of him, really. He'd also known Cassie since she was thirteen, so that probably had a lot to do with it.

'The girl's adamant she's getting into Muse tonight,' I told him. 'Make sure she doesn't.'

'Done,' he agreed instantly. 'You on the pull?'

'Of course. It's been too long, and wrap parties always bring out the *crème de la crème*.' I rubbed my hands together, excited about the prospects of finding a girl to go home with—to her place, mind. I didn't bring girls here. This was my home, and I didn't want to share it with anybody that didn't mean anything to me. Plus, if I went to a girl's place, I could leave before morning without any issues.

'They do seem to bring out the hottest women.'

Clinking noises came from the kitchen. Jackson came and sat on the other sofa in the room, holding a tumbler of whiskey in one hand and the bottle in the other.

'Talking of hot women, what one you got your eye on? I could tell from your voice earlier that there's somebody you're interested in.'

'She's nobody,' he muttered, holding his tumbler in both hands, a contemplative look on his face.

'Nobody, hmm?' I raised an eyebrow. 'I'll be looking out for "nobody" later.'

He chuckled, and I knew I'd got him. Now he'd spend the evening trying to keep me off the scent. Either she was really hot, or the complete opposite, and he was embarrassed about her.

'What time is this thing, anyway?' I asked.

'Starts at seven, but we won't show until at least ten,' he replied. I looked at my watch and grinned at what I saw.

'Well, that's a good thing, seeing as it's six now.'

'It is?' he asked. 'Huh. Guess we better get ready.'

'It's six. We've got a couple of hours before we need to get changed. Is a car picking us up?' It usually did, to ensure the leading star showed up, and to avoid being swarmed by the paps lest they got an unflattering angle of him.

'Yep, the studio's sending one. Gotta have some leading actor perk,' he said.

'Sounds good to me. Now, pour another whiskey and let's discuss my options.'

'Deal.'

Three

Atticus

Being a wallflower had never really bothered me. I understood that Scar needed to network and talk with all the bigwigs who could help her career, but it didn't help me any.

Tugging my dress down for the millionth time in an hour, I wanted the wall to eat me. The green satin number *had* still fit, albeit a bit snug, and Scar had convinced me that this dress would be the one I'd meet my future husband in. Yeah, I hadn't believed her, either.

Nursing a drink, only my second of the night, I felt like a fish out of water. I'd never been much of a drinker, and, as much as I'd been excited by the prospect of a free bar earlier, it was all a little different now that I was actually standing inside Muse.

Scar swanned over to where I was stationed, a small, tentative smile on her face.

'Atti, you really should at least try to mingle,' she said, handing me another drink. 'Oh, look, you're double-parked.'

'Really?' I asked, amused at her tactic to get me to drink more.

'Yep!' She laughed, and started up a chant: 'We like to drink with Atti, 'cause Atti is our mate.'

I rolled my eyes at her, but obviously I had to drink my glass within the count of eight. Them the rules.

'Keep 'em coming!' I shouted at her; the music having got louder within the last few seconds. Or, maybe, now I was actually listening and not just leaning up against a wall.

'You bet,' she said with a chuckle, waving over a waitress who was walking around with a tray of shots. Slowly, the waitress sidled over to where we were standing, a bright smile on her face.

'Hey girls!' she called. 'What you having?'

'What are the choices?' I asked, surveying the tray. There were at least thirty shot glasses, all filled to the brim with a garish liquid. No drink should ever be *that* blue.

'We've got sour cherry, sour blueberry, sour apple and sour watermelon.'

'So, nothing of the non-sour variety?' I asked, and Scar elbowed me in the ribs, shaking her head.

'Don't listen to miss spoilsport here,' she told the waitress. 'We'll take two of each, each.'

'We will?' I asked Scar, looking at her intently. I barely drank, and even one of those shots would send me through the roof.

'Yep, please,' she trilled out. The waitress placed one of each flavour onto the high table to the left of us, making it clear what flavour was what.

'Thank you,' Scar said, and the girl beamed back at her.

'No problem, girls. Let me know if you want more.' She

walked away, swaying her hips as she did so, obviously hoping that she'd catch somebody's eye, or at least the eye of someone who mattered.

'You ready?' Scar asked, handing me one of the green shots with a wicked smile.

'Do I have a choice?'

'Nope,' she said.

'I didn't think so.' I sighed, my shoulders moving up and down with way more force than they should have had.

'Cheers,' she said, clinking her shot glass with mine. I gulped it down, the sour, acrid taste of the alcohol burning my throat on its way down.

Without letting me take a breather, Scar handed me the next one, and then the one after that, and then the one after that.

By the time we'd gulped down all eight each, I'd already started to feel the effects coursing their way through my veins. I wasn't sure of the alcohol content percentage, but the sugar rush they contained probably also had something to do with this new giddiness I was experiencing.

'Want to dance?' Scar asked, reaching out her hand for me to grab onto.

'Eurgh, fine,' I grumbled. 'But if I say stop, you have to let me go back to my wall.'

'Spoilsport.' She wiggled her fingers, and I begrudgingly took them in mine so that she could drag me towards the dancefloor. It was one of those old-fashioned ones from the 80s, all coloured squares and bright lights.

The song changed, and Scar and I caught one another's eye, and smiled wide. Clearly, we were meant to be on the floor right at that moment, because the song that started playing was *our* song. That one song that had got us through all the hard times, and the good times, and all those mediocre times in between. The song was Taio Cruz's *Dynamite*, and every time we heard it play, we had to drop all that we were doing and perform the dance we'd made up as teenagers.

While dancing, I forgot who might be looking at us, and how we were surrounded by the bigwigs of the movie industry. We were just two girls, dancing to our jam, enjoying ourselves. It felt exhilarating.

Once the song ended, and another tune started up, Scar called across to me, 'Atti, there's something I need to tell you.'

'Huh?' I shouted back, not sure that I'd heard her correctly over the music.

'Something I need to tell you!' she tried again, her face one of bad news.

'Nope!' I told her. 'Not happening. I'm finally starting to enjoy this party, so don't you be ruining it for me.' I wagged my pointer finger at her, like a school matron telling off a naughty pupil. Sometimes, I acted way beyond my twenty-six years.

'You sure?' she asked, looking uncertain. Her icy blonde hair had fallen in front of her face, and she quickly brushed it back again. With her red lipstick and cute petite features, she reminded me of a young Marilyn Monroe. That effortless 50s style that she wore when not working suited her perfectly.

'Positive.' And I meant it. No point putting a damper on my evening when it had only just picked up. The alcohol was truly flowing through me now, and a buzz was inside of me, as alive as electricity.

'Okay, then,' she replied, her hands in that placating gesture people made when they were trying to keep you happy. 'Another round, then?'

'Keep 'em coming,' I hollered back.

Once again, she flagged down a staff member, but this one was carrying a tray of champagne.

'Do you think that's a good idea?' I asked, sceptical that sour shots and champers were a good mix of beverages.

'Live a little, girl. You never let your hair down,' she told me, her smile once again wicked and full of sin, and wiggling her hips. Tonight, she was wearing a gorgeous black V-neck, off the shoulder, tea length ball gown, and she looked stunning. Scarlett was one of those girls, who at five foot nine, tried everything she could to own her height, as it had always been something she was self-conscious about.

'Fine, but if I end up with my head half way down a toilet later, I'll be blaming you!' I threatened, but we both knew that I wouldn't do shit to her. I could always blame peer pressure, but really, it would be my fault for going along with it.

'Oh yeah, yeah.' She took two glasses from the tray the waitress was offering, and the two of us sipped and danced, having a good time. We weren't the only ones doing the same, meaning no eyes were on us. Or, rather, me. There were *plenty* of eyes on Scar right now, and I couldn't blame them. She was beautiful.

I was just her sidekick, who felt like a dumpling.

'AND THEN HE told me that if we weren't working on the same project, he'd have asked me out on a date.'

I nodded along to the girl standing in front of us, listening to her words and trying to take them in without giving her my two cents on the situation. Apparently, the lead actor of this film we were here to celebrate had wanted to date her. Yeah, right? Not that I didn't believe he would want to date her, but I also found the whole 'working together' excuse to be a tad flimsy. Plus, you always read in the tabloids about actors, or famous people in general, having a new girl on their arm every week, and I highly doubted this guy was any different.

'Who is he anyway?' I asked, realising that I hadn't asked Scar who she'd been working with. When she first got the role, I'd asked, but she'd told me she wanted to keep it a surprise, which was fine with me, but now, surely, I could find out. The man in question was supposed to be arriving at any moment.

'A grade-A douchebag is who he is,' Scar piped up, her usually happy face souring to one of distaste, like she'd swallowed a fly in her gin and lemonade.

The three of us were no longer on the dancefloor and were standing at the back of the room where the tables were. I'd got a stitch during song twenty, and I needed a breather. We may feel like teenagers, but we certainly couldn't party like them anymore.

'Doesn't tell me much,' I replied, and then sucked down some more of my drink through a paper straw, and paused. *Ew.* I was all for saving the environment, but paper straws always went soggy way too fast, and I ended up with bits of paper in my mouth. And I had an annoying habit of biting the tops of my straws, which drove Scar insane.

'Okay, party people,' the DJ called out through his microphone, and I sniggered at the term 'party people'. What were we? A group of ten-year-old kids at a school disco? 'The leading man is about to arrive, so we want cheers and claps, okay?'

'Bit weird,' I muttered to Scar. 'Surely the guy can enter the wrap party without the VIP treatment? Or is he one of those demanding, diva types?'

Scar rolled her eyes at me.

'I reckon this is something the studio executives think is necessary. It's super lame, whatever way.'

We both nodded our heads in unison, agreeing that this felt more like something you would see at a birthday surprise party than something that should be happening at a big film wrap party.

'Maybe he's got a small dick?' I asked her, and she spat out her drink, unable to keep it in through her laughter.

'You're lucky that didn't just spurt out of my nose!'

'Ladies and gentlemen, the man of the moment...' The DJ was doing his best to hype the room up, but from the looks of the women around me, they didn't need any more reason to be excited. 'Jackson James!'

Cheers and catcalls hit my ears instantly, and I recoiled from the sensory overload. How desperate these women seemed.

I turned my head in the direction of the door and caught my first glimpse of Jackson James in the flesh. I'd seen all of his films, and had followed his career for years, but he definitely was more attractive in the flesh.

'*Phwoar*!' I said in Scar's ear, but she only crossed her arms in defiance, her narrowed eyes still trained on Jackson. And then I saw her gaze falter.

'Er, Atticus, I feel like I really need to tell you something.'

I waved her off, and whispered in her ear, 'You can tell me after this spectacle has ended.'

She nodded, but the tension radiating off of her hadn't

dissipated. There was obviously a story there about her and Jackson that I needed to learn about sometime soon.

Once again, I turned to face the door. Jackson had arrived with another guy, but I couldn't see him properly over the top of a rather tall man standing in front of me. Like in a film, the guy in front of me moved a step to the right, meaning I could get a glimpse of the friend Jackson had arrived with.

No. Way.

Instantly, my insides revolted, and I wanted to get the hell out of dodge. All the alcohol I had consumed was fighting to leave my body, no longer wanting to make a home for itself inside of my stomach.

Of all the bars in the city, why did *Parker Daniels* have to walk into the one I was occupying?

His smug smirk, his stupid eyebrows, and his stupid eyes made me want to stick pins in a voodoo doll of his likeness, and believe me, I'd considered it before...more than I should admit.

I watched as Parker surveyed the room, and I knew I needed to hide. Or duck. Literally anything that would prevent him from seeing me here.

'Excuse me,' I said to the woman we'd been talking to, trying to shove her out of my way so that I could get to the toilets.

Wearing six-inch heels had clearly been one of the worst ideas I could have had, as I stepped to move around the people hovering around the next table over, and I wobbled on the heel. With the next step, I wobbled again, but instead of grabbing the table to right myself, I grabbed the table and took it down with me.

I crashed to the ground with a huge *thud*, and narrowly avoided being crushed by the table. The drinks, however, covered me with an array of smells and colours, now clinging to my skin.

'Shit,' I muttered under my breath.

Trust me to take down a table, and a whole tray of drinks, just because I saw an ex-boyfriend. *The* ex-boyfriend. The one I tried my hardest to forget the existence of.

Wonderful.

Four

Parker

'Over here!'

'Parker! Jackson!'

'Are you happy with your work on *Rules of Engagement,* Jackson?'

'Parker! Do you think you'll be asked to shoot for Bruce King again?'

The two of us turned to each member of the media, flashing them our winning smiles and varying up our poses.

It was a hidden evil of the job, really, but one I'd become quite fond of. I liked having my picture taken, and this was another extension of that.

'Thank you, everybody,' Jackson called out, 'but we really should be heading in now.'

We both gave them a small wave and walked to the entrance of Muse, where two burly bouncers were guarding the door. I'd glanced at the queue on the road when we'd pulled up, and I hadn't seen Cassie or any of her friends, but that didn't mean they weren't in there somewhere.

Or, god forbid, they'd already made it inside somehow.

The bouncers opened the heavy, silver doors for us, and we nodded our thanks. One of the many perks of our jobs was that people were always going out of their way to help. Yeah, yeah, it was a part of what they were paid to do, but still, it felt good to have people cater to you; to wait on you hand and foot.

On entering Muse, the sound of clapping and cheering hit us, like we'd entered a wall of sound and were now surrounded by it. And even though those cheers were for Jackson, I still liked to think that some of them were for me. Especially the later ones that started up, once people had seen who he'd arrived with.

It was a typical party, the studio executives having pulled out all the stops for their main star. Jackson was good-naturedly smiling and waving, keeping up the appearance that he enjoyed all of this attention, but I knew that deep down he found it all uncomfortable. I was the one who really flourished under the spotlight. After all. The light loved me.

I surveyed the room, taking in all the corners, trying to find myself a hot piece of woman to lay the foundation with. I'd figured out by now what to look for when sizing up a one-night stand.

A commotion took place near the back of the room, and I watched amused as a woman who (on catching sight of me) had darted away, only to lose her balance in her skyscraper heels and had grabbed a table for support. I gave a small chuckle as the woman toppled over and the entire table and its contents went down with her, like the Titanic and its captain.

A chorus of 'WAYYYYY!' went up from around the room,

everybody now having clocked that some poor soul was laid flat out on the floor. I tried my best to hide my smug grin, but really, the whole thing had inflated my ego. I'd had a few women faint at the sight of me before, but I'd never had anybody stumble and fall quite as spectacularly as this girl had.

Without thinking, I headed in the direction of the woman, hoping that I could help her stand, or at least offer to buy her a drink.

Actually, it was a free bar. So, I could at least offer to *get* her a drink.

As I got closer, I realised that the girl seemed overly familiar to me. She'd covered her face with her hands, due to embarrassment I assumed, but there was something tugging at my brain that I couldn't place.

Had I slept with her before?

Or maybe she'd been a conquest I'd never been able to land. That would explain why she'd darted at the mere sight of me. Although, they were rare specimens.

'Are you okay?' I asked, crouching down closer to her, so that I didn't feel like a giant staring down at her splayed out on the alcohol covered floor.

'Fucking wonderful,' the girl growled, and I knew I recognised that voice.

'Atticus?' I squinted, looking at the hair and the body I could see, and trying to figure out whether the face hidden behind those hands was one I thought I'd never see again.

'Yep,' she grunted, the sound muffled through her hands. 'Now, go away.'

'I came over here to help,' I told her, amused that she thought I'd just walk away now that I knew it was her. Little did she know, I still fantasised about her and what we'd had together. She was the one who got away, and I'd never been able to explain to her the full truth...that I'd never cheated on her with Alexa that night, no matter what she thought she saw.

'Mhm. Of course you did. You're such a gentleman, P. Piss off, so that I can get up without having to know that you saw me during this shame spiral.'

I laughed, overjoyed to be hearing her voice again, even if she clearly wanted nothing to do with me.

Atticus Allman had been my girl from the time we were fifteen and she'd agreed to go on a date with me, and even though we hadn't seen each other in over five years, I still thought of her as *mine*. A part of me believed that I always would.

'Shame spiral, huh?' I joked, watching as she slowly removed her hands from her face to reveal a very red, and very mad, expression underneath.

'Eurgh. Haven't you left yet?'

A crowd had formed around us, but nobody was trying to help Atticus. They were mostly there to listen to our conversation and watch the drama unfold.

'Why would I do that? I'd miss your face turning the perfect shade of red.'

'Glad to see you're still a massive prick,' she sputtered out. I thrust my hand forward, hoping that she'd grab it in hers so that she could at least move to sitting. The fact that Atticus was still laying on the floor of the club meant that people had started to take pictures, and some were probably live streaming her pity party. She'd always been clumsy; we used to joke around about how she was one of the only people around that could trip on air.

'Me?' I swept my hand away from her to hold it against my chest.

'Yes, you,' she spat, as she moved herself to sitting without any help from me. You'd have thought that my hand was poisonous the way she'd been glaring at it. 'Urgh, my dress.'

I looked her up and down, starting at her head and travelling all the way to her heels, and I liked what I saw. Atticus had always been curvy, and even though she'd been self-conscious about it, it was a part of her that I loved. Her tits were the perfect handful, and her arse was perfectly rounded. My dick came to life, sensing that *the one* was around, and I had to change my position slightly, otherwise Atticus would sit up into a face full of my crotch. Crap. My dick liked that imagery a little *too* much.

'Everything okay over here?' Jackson asked, joining the fray. Really, I should stand up, but my crouching position was helping to hide my *situation*. The livestreams, and the people watching them, would never let me forget if I gave them that.

'Oh, totally fine.' Atticus waved her hand around, and I smiled. She always had been a gesticulator. That word sounded a lot dirtier than it should, and I had to start thinking about my dog and other mundane things, otherwise I'd be crouching all night. 'This arsehole here hasn't offered to help me up.'

Jackson looked down at me, one eyebrow raised (a move the press called the *Jackson Quirk*), and I tilted my head towards Atticus slightly. He seemed to understand what I meant, but I thought I'd make it clear.

'*Atticus* here is clearly suffering from a concussion as well as smelling like a piss-up in a brewery.'

Jackson's eyes gleamed with knowledge, and he clocked on pretty fast. There'd been many a drunken night where I'd opened my big mouth and told him about my regrets with her. He knew the truth too, which made two out of the three of us.

'Well, Atticus, how about I help you instead?' he asked, bending slightly and holding out his hand for her to hold. What a wanker.

'Thank you,' she said, grabbing his large hand with her tiny one, happily letting him help her up. 'Now that's how you charm a lady.'

Finally, I stopped crouching and stood up to my full height, making sure that I didn't slouch.

Atticus turned her blazing blue eyes to me, and if at any part of this conversation I'd believed that maybe she would hear me out, her look now let me know otherwise. With the force of a thousand fires, her glare was filled with every ounce of hatred she still held for me.

The dress looked a lot better on her standing, the green slinky material sticking to all of her curves, and her hourglass figure was on full display.

'Atticus!' A girl rushed up, frantically, to where the three of us were. The group around us hadn't disappeared. If anything, it had grown now that Jackson had joined us. The guy attracted attention wherever he went, and I was happy enough in my sexuality to admit that the guy was a good-looking dude.

'Scarlet?' I blurted out, recognising the girl who had just flown at us now that she was facing me. Taking her in, I saw that actually she hadn't changed much since the last time I'd seen her, except that right now she wasn't shouting at me, so that was a plus.

She narrowed her eyes at me, and spat out, 'Parker.'

Hm, guessed she was still holding a grudge, too. Made sense. The two of them had been the best of friends for years, and although it surprised me that they were still friends, I understood it.

'Well, as fun as this is...' Atticus said, once again glaring at me. 'Thank you, Jackson.'

'No problem, darling.' The evil fucker had a glint in his eye, and I knew that he was trying to get a rise out of me. 'Let me get us a round of drinks.'

He called over to somebody, and they dropped what they were doing to get him what he wanted. I chuckled.

'What you laughing about, dickhead?' Scarlet crossed her arms, frowning at me, and I raised the corner of my lips to further enrage her. Even when Atticus and I had been happy together, Scar and I hadn't always seen eye to eye.

'The sour look on your face, Scar. Clearly not getting any.'

'Oh, so you all know each other, then?' Jackson asked, as if he didn't know. It was at moments like this that I remembered the guy was a bloody great actor. The girls would believe that he had no clue about what was happening here.

'Sadly,' Atticus said, deadpan. 'We all went to school together.'

'And how do you know Parker?' Scarlet asked Jackson, looking between us both. He looked at me, and I shrugged, letting him take the lead here.

'House share. This loser moved in and I haven't been able to get rid of him since. I've tried.'

'Oh, ha, ha, mate.' Swift as a panther, I wrapped my arm

around his neck and got him in a headlock. No matter where we were, event or at home, we never changed the way we acted. It was part of our brand. We were constantly being flouted in the media as the type of guys other men wanted to be mates with, and the kind of guys girls would want to take home to their mum—but probably not their dad.

I let him go, and he chuckled darkly. I'd won this round, but I knew that I needed to steer him away from these two soon, otherwise he'd open his big mouth and tell them something I didn't need them, or the large crowd that *still* hadn't got bored and disappeared, knowing

'Unlucky for you,' Atticus told him, sounding like she actually meant it, which did hurt a little. Her gaze was sympathetic, and I huffed at her theatrics. She turned her eyes to me at the noise, and spat, 'What now?'

'Oh, nothing. Just wondered how long you were going to stand there making the place look untidy.'

'Making the place look untidy?' Her venomous words were almost palpable, the intensity of them hitting me square in the chest. 'God, I hate you.'

'You're cutting me deep, Atti.' I placed my hand over my heart, smiling widely. Using her nickname hadn't been a conscious decision, and I could see instantly that it had made things worse.

'You. Do. Not. Get. To. Call. Me. Atti.'

In between each word, she poked me in the chest, hard, really driving her point home. She was trying to make me mad, but with each poke, I had to stop myself from getting hard at her touch. I couldn't blame the guy. He'd stopped thinking that having Atticus's touch was a possibility.

'What *do* I get to call you?' I asked, pushing my luck, but getting a kick out of it, nonetheless.

'You don't get to call me. Period,' she said, anger in her glare. With her parting words, Atticus grabbed Scar's arm in hers, and turned slightly, before turning back and adding, 'Thank you, Jackson.'

When the girls were out of earshot, Jackson started to laugh in earnest, amused at how that had just played out.

'So, that's *the* Atticus then?' he asked.

'How many girls do you know walking around going by the name of Atticus?' I asked in return.

'Surprisingly, none.' A waitress came up to us, holding a tray with drinks, and I looked her up and down, hoping that I'd like what I saw. She seemed nice enough, and she had a great rack, but seeing Atticus had done a number on my head. 'She seemed pissed at you though.'

'Course she did. Not like she's ever listened to the truth.'

'If that was anything to go by, I doubt she'll be listening to you anytime soon, mate. Commiserations.'

I wanted to joke back, tell him how wrong he was, or tell him how I'd have Atticus underneath me within the month, but I couldn't. Even I knew that the latter was a pipe dream.

'Alright, wanker, no need to rub it in.'

Finishing off my whiskey, I took another from the tray the waitress had left on the table for us. The table that had been on the floor after Atticus's fall, but had been rescued and returned to an upright position.

Glancing around the room, I saw that finally the crowd had dissipated from around us. The odd straggler still held their phone up in our direction, but that was all a part of the norm now, and I held up my glass for him to clink with his.

'Congrats, bro.'

'Cheers,' he replied. We both took a sip. 'So, seemed like you knew Scarlet pretty well? She been friends with Atticus for some time?'

'Forever,' I said, sceptical as to why he'd be asking. Then, like a light bulb in my mind, it clicked. 'Oh, so *she's* the girl, ay?'

'Piss off,' he said good-naturedly. 'She's pretty cool.'

'She's a pain in the arse.'

'Hm. Either way, what you going to do about Atticus?'

'You think I should do something?' I asked, but really, I just wanted him to confirm what I'd already decided. There was no way I was going to let her walk away that easily. Not now that I'd seen her again.

'Stop fishing. I know you've already got it into your head that you want to get her to hear you out.'

'Can you blame me?' I spotted Atticus and Scarlet over by the bar, sitting on stools, deep in conversation. Reckon I knew what they were talking about.

'Nope. All the luck to you, mate.' He held out his glass to me, and I clinked mine with his.

'Thanks. Think I'm gonna need it.'

'Oh, that woman is going to make you work for it.'

'You have no idea,' I replied.

If I knew Atticus, and I was pretty certain that I did, then I knew that she would make me jump through plenty of hoops to even get out a greeting. She'd been blindsided tonight, and hadn't expected to see me, but now that she had, I wanted to make sure that she didn't forget my face.

'I've got faith in you,' he said, patting me on my shoulder.

'But if you want to try to talk to her tonight, you might want to make your move. Looks to me like she's leaving.'

Atticus was hugging Scarlet, and after she moved away, she waved at her slightly. I watched, frozen to the spot, as she put on a coat that covered all of her curves, and did nothing to flatter her.

I hadn't expected her to leave before I could talk to her again, so I hadn't fully formed a game plan in my mind.

Looked like I'd have to act on impulse.

Wonderful.

'Eurgh, did you see that smug face of his? Looking like he deserved to be talking to me,' I said to Scar once we'd moved away from the guys.

'Actually, he looked pretty happy to see you,' she said, ever the diplomat. 'Even in the short time I was there, I saw him check you out at least twice.'

'He was probably staring at the stains on my dress,' I grumbled. 'Or maybe he was looking at me and comparing how plain I was in comparison to the girls he pulls now.'

'I highly doubt that, doll. He *definitely* liked what he was looking at.'

'There's no way for you to know that for sure,' I told her, trying to ignore the fluttering of hope in my belly. A large part of me hoped that he had been checking me out and had been kicking himself at what he was missing out on. He could still have this, have me, if he hadn't ruined everything so exponentially.

'Stop thinking in big words,' Scar told me, taking a sip of her cocktail, a mischievous smile playing on her lips.

'How'd you know I was?' I asked and drained my glass. Calling across the bar, I told the man there, 'Keep 'em coming.' He nodded and started filling a cocktail shaker with only he knew what. After the embarrassing fall, and no doubt the many subsequent clips online, I wanted to forget it had even happened, and the only way to do that was through copious amounts of alcohol.

'Your face always scrunches up funny when you're thinking super hard.'

'It does not,' I protested, a little too vehemently, and Scar raised her eyebrow.

'Keep telling yourself that, hun, if it makes you feel better.'

'Do not "hun" me, you bitch,' I said with a fake gasp. Scarlet had the tendency to use names such as 'hun', 'babes', 'girl', and more when drinking. It was definitely a sign that her loose lips were out, and would probably land her in hot water before the night was out.

'Want me to go over there and tell Parker you still want him?' She made to get up off her stool, and I instantly threw my arm out to block her from leaving.

'Don't you dare,' I said, only removing my arm from her path when she sat back down again. 'Anyway, it would be a lie.'

'Hmm,' was all she said, and I didn't like the sound of scepticism in her hum.

'What?' I asked. At the same time, the bartender appeared at our end of the bar with two cocktails.

'Pardon?' he asked, and I waved him off.

'Sorry, was asking her.' I hitched my thumb in Scarlet's

direction, and he nodded in understanding. With a wide smile, he left to serve somebody else. 'He's cute.'

'That guy?' she asked, looking back in his direction for a second look. 'Not my type.'

'Well, I guess he's no Jackson James,' I said, offhandedly, hoping that she'd take the bait I just offered. As usual, she didn't disappoint.

'I do *not* like Jackson James,' she scoffed, and then added, 'and why does everybody call him by his full name like he's so bloody special? Is the name Jackson not pretentious enough?'

'I can't exactly comment on pretentious names,' I said, thinking about an article I'd once read. 'Did you know Atticus topped a list of most pretentious baby names?'

'Wow, Atti. What a fun fact. So glad I invited you out,' she deadpanned. I hit her knee with mine, and she laughed. 'And let me guess. Jackson wasn't on the list?'

'Nope, not that I can recall.' I finished my drink and grabbed the other. Scar hadn't touched it yet, so that made it mine in my book. 'Was this what you wanted to tell me?'

'Huh?' She looked at me, all dazed and confused.

'Was Parker being here what you wanted to talk to me about?'

'Oh,'—her eyes widened, then she opened and closed her mouth a couple of times—'no.' She took a sip of her cocktail, her face scrunched up, making her resemble a cute-looking pixie. 'Never mind what I was gonna say. It's no biggie.'

'If you're sure,' I said, scepticism rife in my tone. She'd been pretty insistent about it earlier.

'Don't look over,' Scar leaned in a little and whispered, 'but the boys are looking in this direction.'

'Huh?' I asked loudly, and I glanced around. Scar shushed me, holding her finger up to her lips.

'Parker's looking over here,' she whispered, her eyes bugging out of her face as she tried to convey her meaning. 'Reckon they're talking about you?' Her tone was hopeful, and I had to nip that in the bud before she got any ideas.

'Not going there, Scar. Also, weren't you just acting like a cow to him twenty minutes ago?'

'Oh, that,' she fobbed it off with a wave of her hand, 'you know that's how I've always been with him. Love/hate relationship and all that.'

'It should definitely be one of hate. You know what he did to me.'

Her face and tone sobered up in an instant, and she hushed out, 'I'm sorry. I *do* hate him for what he did to you. I've got your back, girl.'

I glanced over and saw that Parker and Jackson were indeed looking in our direction. Jackson's gaze was on my best friend, appraisal in his gaze, and I filed that little tid-bit away for later.

'I think I'm gonna go,' I blurted out, having made the decision in that instant. 'I can't be here around him. I'm sorry, Scar.'

'I get it. Want me to come with you?' she asked, already waving somebody over to ask them to grab my coat.

'No!' I told her, meaning it. 'You. Stay. Enjoy. This is your night.'

'I was an extra who had a total of two lines.'

'And what a wonderful two lines they'll be,' I told her, giving her a swift kiss on the cheek, and a brief hug. I waved awkwardly and then laughed at myself. Why on earth was I waving to her? We lived together now, and I'd be seeing her when she got in.

A worker handed me my coat, and I put it on, wanting to leave as fast as I could without moving too speedily. I didn't need to fall flat again—I'd already had enough embarrassment tonight to last me a long time.

Moving slowly, yet effectively, I managed to get outside into the fresh, brisk air without bumping into anybody, or falling over, so I considered that to be a great achievement. I pulled out my phone and arranged a lift home before placing it back in my bag. Pacing up and down the pavement to keep warm, I kept my head down. The queue to get into Muse wrapped around the corner, and I was surprised that they were even planning on letting the public in. Or maybe they weren't, and this was all a marketing ploy to make the place look like the best place to be.

'Atticus?' A young, female voice called out, and I looked around, trying to find where it had come from. Who on earth would be calling me, outside of Muse, in all places? I had one of those names that it was rare that I heard it being called, and it *wasn't* for me. It wasn't like when a teacher had called out "George!" and five kids had answered.

'Behind you,' the voice said, and I slowly pivoted on my foot to look behind me. A teenager, no older than eighteen, was standing there beaming at me.

Surely not.

'Cassie?' I asked, recognition coming to me. The brown hair and blue eyes looked familiar and even though I hadn't seen her since she was twelve, I just knew that it was her.

'Yeah!' she said enthusiastically. 'My am I so happy to see you!'

She wrapped her tiny arms around me and pulled me into the biggest bear hug. Warmth filled me at the reception I was receiving from her. I'd always got along well with Parker's family, but after we'd split up, I hadn't felt comfortable around any of them anymore. It would have been odd to stay friendly with them when their son, or brother, had broken my heart.

'How are you?' she gushed, stepping back to take me in from head to toe. 'You look amazing. Have you just come out from Muse?'

I nodded, overwhelmed by her, but smiling nonetheless. She was no longer that gangly teenager who had bothered us to play games with her and had pestered me to braid her hair.

'I'm good, thanks. You look amazing! Honestly, Cass, you've really grown into those limbs of yours.' We both laughed at that. 'Yeah, I did. You remember my friend Scarlet? She has a small role in the film.'

'Awesome! I tried to convince P to get me in, but he wouldn't budge. You know how much of a spoil sport he can be.' She pouted, but then livened up again. 'Is Jackson inside?'

'Yep,' I told her, finding her crush on him amusing. No wonder Parker hadn't wanted her to come to Muse tonight. 'I'm sure if your brother knew you were standing out here freezing in such a skimpy dress he'd get you in.'

'Pft,' she scoffed, 'you'd think so, wouldn't you? But nope. He's been no fun since you left.'

I bristled a little at that, but I held my tongue, not wanting to sour the conversation. I'd always wondered just what he'd told his family, and if Cass believed that I'd left, then he clearly hadn't been very truthful.

'Not cool.' We fell silent for a moment, but then I had an idea. 'Hey, how about I text Scar and see if she can get you in?'

'Would you?' She smiled with relief, and I wondered how long she and her friends had been standing here for. I messaged Scar, who said to tell them to come to the door in ten, and she'd take them in.

'Meet Scar at the door in ten, and you're in,' I told her.

'You're the best!' she said, grabbing me once again in another tight hug. I smiled, and like an unusual old lady, I took a quick sniff of her head, taking in the scent that was Cassie.

'Er, Atti.' She pulled back and raised her brows at me. 'Did you just smell my head?'

'Shhhh,' I hushed. 'Pretend it never happened.'

We both chuckled, and I quickly looked away from her (all too knowing) gaze. Then I saw her eyes light up even more, and I knew what was about to happen next. Could I not catch a break?

'Atticus!' Parker called, and I knew that by putting my previous question out into the universe, I'd clearly jinxed myself.

I groaned, hoping that Parker would get the hint that I was *not* interested in turning around, or in hearing whatever words he thought I needed to hear. Believe me, I didn't need to hear any of them. Not now, and not ever.

'Well, I really must be off. My lift should be here soon. It's been great to see you,' I told Cassie, ignoring her brother. 'Have a wonderful evening.'

'Can we catch up soon?' she asked, her eyes wide and her lips in a playful pout. Nice to see that not everything had changed.

'Sure,' I said with a chuckle, and handed her my phone. 'Put your number in and message yourself.'

Cassie did as I said and handed it back to me. I could sense

Parker was still standing there, wanting to grab my attention, but I wouldn't look at him. I *couldn't.* My resolve was only so strong, although I was brave enough to admit to myself that he looked mighty fine this evening.

'Well, I best be off,' I said with a small wave at Cass. Turning around, while still avoiding Parker's eye, I walked around the corner in hopes that my ride would be there. I took my phone out of my pocket and checked the app. *Shit.* He'd cancelled on me. Some lame excuse about being too far away, which made no sense, as the driver had been the one to accept the job in the first place.

'Eurgh!' I shouted out in frustration. Could this night get any worse?

'You okay?' Parker asked, and I internally pinched myself. I must stop putting questions out there that don't need to be answered.

What could happen next? Parker offering me a ride home?

'Do you need a lift?' he asked, as if hearing my internal thoughts.

'Not from you,' I spat out, still looking every way that wasn't him. I sensed his next move before he made it, so that when he came to stand directly in front of me, I was already looking down at the ground. Petty? Yes. Satisfying? Kind of.

'How are you getting home then?' he asked, and I wanted to put him in his place, but really I didn't have a great answer for him.

'I don't know,' I said, 'but you've been drinking, so you can't take me home, anyway.'

Finally, I looked up, as I'd been feeling like a bit of an idiot staring at the ground while having this conversation. It hadn't felt natural, and really, I was probably making myself look like even more of a tit than I already had this evening. Who knew, there could be paparazzi around trying to get a picture of Parker—or worse, there could be wannabe famous people with smartphones trying to capture something newsworthy to make a quick fifty quid from a gossip rag.

'I didn't drive here,' he said with a smug smile. 'The studio sent a car.'

'Well, oooh, how exciting for you. Must feel good to be so wanted and adored.'

'It isn't bad,' he said, shrugging, and all I wanted to do was punch him. That would knock that smug look off of his too-perfect face. It wasn't fair that he'd aged well. His boyish features were now all man, and if I didn't stop my train of thought, I'd be fanning myself in mere minutes. 'So, let me arrange a car for you.'

'Fine,' I snapped, because it really *was* very cold, and I wanted to snuggle down in my duvet and sleep off the shame. 'But you are *not* getting in the car.'

I pointed my finger at him and jabbed him in the chest a couple of times for good measure. This wasn't me accepting an olive branch, or anything of the sort. I wanted to get home, and he was offering a solution to that problem; nothing more.

He held up his hands in a placating gesture, and said, 'Okay, Mardy.'

A growl made its way up my throat, and before I could hold it back, it left my mouth and I saw him flinch.

'What did you just call me?' I asked, knowing I'd heard him correctly, but wanting to see if he'd repeat it. Really, I was goading him into it, and knowing him the way I did, I knew he'd walk straight into it.

He had the gall to look cocky, even knowing that he'd overstepped the mark, and that I was three seconds away from attempting to rip his head off.

'Mardy,' he said again, plain and simple. He was trying to get a rise out of me, and stupid girl that I was, I was letting him!

'I am not mardy, but if you don't arrange me a lift within the next ten minutes, then you'll see just how mardy I can truly be.'

'Woah, hold your horses.' He got out his phone and tapped away a message that I really hoped was for a driver. It buzzed in his hand, and he said, 'The car will be pulling up out front in two minutes.'

'Thank you,' I said begrudgingly, because even if I hated him, I still had enough manners to thank somebody when they helped me. My parents had raised me to always say thanks, but at times, like now, it was more of a curse.

'No problem. Are you sure I can't twist your arm? I'd really like to talk to you,' Parker said, his voice lower than it had been all evening. It was sensual, and it touched me *there.* He knew I loved a low, sinful voice.

'Not going to happen,' I said, 'and if you'll excuse me, there's a car pulling up out front for me.'

The smile remained on his face, but his eyes narrowed slightly as he ran his fingers through his hair.

'I really think you should reconsider,' he said, taking a step towards me.

'Is that a threat?' I asked, feigning shock. I knew he didn't mean it to come across as menacing, and really it hadn't, but I needed to get away from his presence. Even just being around his cedar-wood scent was making my synapses malfunction.

'This isn't the end of it, you know,' he replied casually,

ignoring my question. He reached out to brush a strand of hair out of my face, and I shivered at the heat of his touch. He leaned forward and brushed his lips against my ear. 'You will hear me out.'

Like I'd been struck, I stepped back, nearly losing my balance when my heel got caught in a crack in the pavement. I wobbled, grabbing out to hold on to anything to prevent myself from landing on my arse on the ground. Unlucky for me, the only thing there was to grab was Parker, and although I'd been aiming to grab onto his arms, I actually ended up grabbing his waist and pulling him forward with the motion.

So, there I was, half bent over, with my face in my ex-boyfriend's crotch. And to top it off, I heard a click, and saw the flash of a paparazzi's camera catching the moment on film.

Fucking fantastic.

Six

Parker

I woke up the morning after the wrap party with a pounding headache.

After I'd seen Atticus safely into the studio car, I headed straight back inside to have another whiskey—or ten.

And then, just when I believed that my night couldn't get much worse, I saw Cassie and her friends hanging out with Scarlet, and a large group of men, meaning that somehow Atticus and Scar had managed to override Jackson's demands. Really, I shouldn't have been that surprised. My sister was a determined and headstrong girl when she set her mind to something, and if I knew anything about Atticus and Scarlet, it was that they always tried to sway the universe in their direction.

My plans of leaving the party with a beautiful woman on my arm had been dashed the moment I saw Atticus fall, and I hadn't been in the mood for a random, meaningless hook-up after she'd gone.

She'd really thrown me off of my game, and as much as I wanted to be irritated by that, I couldn't. This was *my* Atti we were talking about.

Grumbling, I got out of bed and stumbled into the sitting room to let Radley out of his crate. When he was a puppy, it had made sense to crate-train him for the night time, and now that he was older, he didn't want to sleep anywhere else. Which I was thankful for really, as although I did have a super king-size bed, Radley would take up all the space in an instant.

'Morning, boy,' I said, smiling when I saw how excited he was to see me. That was one thing I loved about having a dog. Knowing that he loved me and wanted to be around me all the time made me feel good about myself. A dog's love was unconditional, and truly, Radley was a man's best friend. I crouched down and unlocked the door so that he could get out. He enthusiastically showed me some love, and then trotted over to the kitchen, knowing the routine. I followed behind him and entered the kitchen and grabbed the necessary items needed to feed the big lump that was sitting patiently at my feet.

I placed down his bowl of food and watched as he devoured it, like a dog starved, as I waited for my pot of coffee to percolate. Honestly, you'd think he never ate the way he scoffed it down, and then looked up at you with wide eyes, pleading for more.

'Morning,' Jackson grumbled, coming into the kitchen and putting the kettle on. Jackson was a tea drinker, and we often disagreed over who had the better beverage in the morning. Either way, the caffeine lived in our veins. 'Y'alright?'

'Could be better,' I said, noticing the dark circles underneath his eyes. 'Guess I could say the same to you.'

'Don't remind me,' he said, rubbing at his still bloodshot eyes. 'I barely slept. Couldn't stop thinking about everything.'

'Like what?' I asked, picking up my coffee mug to blow on it. I hated adding cold water to make it cool down, because then I forgot I'd done that and left it too long, and ended up drinking coffee that wasn't cold enough to be classed as an iced coffee, but wasn't warm either. I drank it black, too, which meant that I didn't even have the milk to cool it down some.

Jackson was the opposite. The milkier his tea, the better. It was a waste of a tea bag if you asked me, the way he left it in there for all of two seconds, and then quickly fished it out again. If the tabloids got a hold of that news, then there'd be uproar. Us Brits took tea very seriously, and the country would be up in arms if they knew one of their most beloved actors did the tradition dirty like that.

'Like the fact that I've invited Scarlet and Atticus over here for dinner tonight,' he said, looking sheepish.

'You've done what now?' I asked, wondering if I'd heard him wrong. Surely he hadn't just said that he'd invited Atticus to dinner. In our space. Tonight.

'Hear me out,' he said, his tone placating. 'I didn't know when I invited her that she was Atticus.'

'Bullshit,' I blurted out, 'like you know many girls named Atticus.'

'Mate, I invited Scarlet, and she asked if she could bring her best friend. How was I to know that her best friend was Atticus?'

'And when did you extend this invitation?' I asked, wondering if he'd asked her yesterday before the wrap party or after, because if it was after—or even during—then the man was lying.

'On set yesterday, before we'd wrapped. Scarlet wants to improve her chances of landing a main role, and I said I'd help her. I thought a dinner here might be a better way to get to know her a little better, and when she asked to bring a friend, I wanted to make her feel at ease.'

'Of course you want to get to know her a little better,' I said, wagging my finger at him. 'She's quite the looker.'

'She's beautiful, yes, but not my type at all.' His tone was certain, and I wondered what she'd done to make him feel so strongly about it.

'A beautiful girl who isn't your type? Never thought I'd hear the day,' I joked, and we both knew it was a joke, because no matter how often the press reported that Jackson was sleeping around, it simply wasn't true. He just kept up the illusion that that was the case to keep the reporters off his back.

'So, are they coming?'

'Huh?' he asked, taking a seat at the breakfast bar with his mug of tea. 'Oh, well, I've not heard otherwise, although now I reckon Scarlet might have to work harder to get Atticus to agree.'

'True. Not like she'd have known we were mates, or that we lived together.' I shrugged. 'Message her and ask.'

'Alright, mate. Let me at least finish my morning caffeine fix before I start grovelling on your behalf.'

I leaned up against the kitchen side, nursing my mug in my hands. Radley, who had realised he wasn't going to get any more food, had gone back to lay in his crate.

'Well, I doubt she'll come,' I told him, meaning to end it there, but found myself spilling the entire events of the previous evening. He listened in silence, nodding in the right places, and once I'd finished, he smiled.

'So, she didn't give you the time of day?' he asked, knowing the answer.

'Basically, yeah, but she exchanged numbers with my sister, no problem.' She'd looked so happy catching up with Cassie, especially before I'd joined them. When I walked out of Muse and saw them there, chatting away like old times, my heart twinged slightly. For years after we split up, Cassie had asked when she'd get to see Atti again. It broke my heart having to tell her she'd probably never see her again.

Jackson clearing his throat brought me back to the now.

'Your sister didn't break her heart,' he reminded me, and I grunted.

'I'm aware, arsehole.' I threw a cloth at him, chuckling when it landed in the centre of his face. 'Imma go shower. Let me know when you hear back from Scar.'

'Fine, but don't be surprised if it isn't good news.'

'Convince her,' I told him, looking sternly at him. 'Get her here, even if you have to lie and tell her I won't be home.'

'I'll see what I can do,' he said, raising his eyebrow sceptically.

I put my mug into the sink and left him at the breakfast bar, hoping that he'd be texting Scar and getting the girls here for dinner tonight.

I just needed an opportunity to speak to her. A moment alone to clear up the past. She had no real clue about what really happened, and I understood why it had all looked so bad, but I needed to clear it all up.

Then, maybe, just maybe, I'd be able to convince her to give me a second chance.

The afternoon passed, and I hadn't heard anything more from Jackson about whether the girls were coming or not. I hoped he'd be able to convince them, because even though I played it cool last night and let her leave without too much of an objection, I did really want her to hear me out. I'd taken Radley on a walk, and so far, all I had done was wonder about how I would approach the topic of the past if I did get a chance to talk to Atti alone.

How did you tell a stubborn woman that she was wrong? And that she'd been wrong for six long years. Six years that the two of us could have been happy and settled.

Maybe I wouldn't lead with that point. She was known to have a temper, and I didn't need to piss her off before she heard what I wanted to say.

My phone buzzed, and I grabbed it out of my pocket, trying my best to keep Radley from pulling and causing me to lose my balance. He got super excited on walks, and being such a big dog, he could easily overpower me if he wanted to.

'Y'ello?' I answered, sure as shit, hoping that Jackson was calling with good news.

'They're in,' he said, simple and to the point. I smiled wide, feeling the tide turning in my favour. Atticus wouldn't know what had hit her when I turned on my charm. She'd fallen for it once, so there was no reason why she wouldn't again.

'What time are they coming?' I asked, running through how much time there would be to freshen up and change; time to make myself look as irresistible as possible.

'I told Scar to come for eight. They usually prompt?' he asked, and my mind went back to a time when we were eighteen, and Scar and Atti threw a joint birthday party. People had started to arrive at seven, yet the two of them didn't make their appearance until gone nine. They'd chatted crap about how they wanted to make an entrance and arrive fashionably late, but really, I knew it was because their hair and make-up had taken longer than they'd anticipated.

I chuckled, and told Jackson, 'We'll be lucky if we see them before ten.'

'Seriously?' he grumbled, and I knew he was considering uninviting them. He hated eating too late, saying that it messed with his sleep and peace.

'Narh, mate, I'm just kidding. They'll be half an hour late, tops.'

'Thinking of cooking Italian, do they like that?'

'Who doesn't like that?' I asked, my mouth already watering at the thought of Jackson's meatballs. Huh. Maybe I shouldn't say that anywhere outside of my mind; people might get the wrong idea. 'Atti's a vegetarian though, so no meat.'

'Reckon she still is? It's been a few years since you spoke to her about her meat preferences.'

'Oh, ha, ha. There's no way she would have changed her mind. She's as stubborn as they come, remember?'

'True,' he pondered for a moment longer, 'any requests?'

The perfect way to get Atticus on board hit me, and I knew exactly how I could convince her that I still knew her, still knew something she liked.

'There's a spinach and mascarpone tagliatelle recipe that Atticus adores. I'll find it for you.'

'Okay, but you need to let me know soon so that I can get the things delivered,' he told me. I nodded, then realised he couldn't actually see me.

'Sounds good to me, mate. I'll be back in ten.'

'See you soon.'

I hung up and focused on walking again. Lucky for me, I hadn't walked into any streetlights while I'd been on the phone. My mind had travelled so far that I wouldn't have noticed if anybody had been in my path, or if Radley had tried to make a break for it.

I couldn't even smell Atticus's strawberry and vanilla scent, yet my mind was occupied with thoughts of her.

With an extra pep in my step, Radley and I finished our walk and made our way back to the apartment. There had been no paparazzi, and no girls throwing themselves at me, so I took the day as a success. I understand how big-headed it sounded, that I believed the media would want to get a picture of me, or that women would throw themselves at me, but honestly, you'd be surprised at how often it happened. Or maybe you wouldn't, but it really did happen a lot. It was the life I'd inadvertently signed up for when I became a highly paid model and moved in with Jackson.

My career had taken off after Atticus and I had split up, as I'd only done a few shoots before the drama happened. I wondered what she thought about it all; whether she was proud of me, or whether she wondered why I had continued modelling after that day.

Either way, I felt good about my chances over the course of the evening. We'd be eating her favourite food, and if I played my cards right, I reckoned I could get her alone.

Honestly, I felt fantastic, actually.

Real fucking fantastic.

Seven

Atticus

'We can't go!' I shouted at Scar for the umpteenth time.

All I'd done all day was tell her that we couldn't attend dinner at the boys' place. She'd got home in the real early hours of the morning, waking me up as she stumbled all over the place trying to take her heels off.

Clearly, somebody had had a better evening than me. Wasn't hard though, seeing as Scarlet hadn't been captured sprawled out on Muse's floor, *or* with her face in her ex-boyfriend's crotch.

When I first woke up, I'd tentatively called up a popular tabloid website on my phone called *Hive Mind*, and winced when my own face greeted me. Or what would have been my face if it hadn't been covered with my hands, or Parker's body.

Had I really looked that bad in that dress?

And did my coat really make me look that old?

I'd thrown my phone across my room in a strop, and it had landed in one of the many boxes that still littered the floor.

Many people talked of how a cluttered area means a cluttered mind, but for me, that had never really rung true. My mind was cluttered, yeah, but it had *nothing* to do with the state of my bedroom.

'We have to go!' she shouted back, her eyes blazing at me from across the living room, the sofa in between us acting as a barrier. A battle line of sorts. 'I've told Jackson we'll be there.'

'Then *untell* him!' I said, fully emphasising my point by gesticulating wildly. My hands took on a life of their own when I was mad, and the fact that Scar had tried to blindside me with a dinner with Parker made me *really* mad.

'No can do,' she said with glee, and I frowned at her.

'You don't even like Parker,' I told her, suspicious of her intentions. She *knew* how he'd treated me, and just exactly what had gone down back then, so I couldn't understand why Scar was forcing this dinner so much.

'I don't hate the dude,' she said with a shrug. The moment she caught my gaze, she wilted slightly under it, like a flower who hadn't seen enough sunlight, or had been forgotten about and never watered. '*Yes,* he did you wrong, and we know it, but don't you want to go tonight and flaunt just how well put together your life is now? Wouldn't that be satisfactory?'

'It *would* be a major eff you,' I pondered, seeing the benefits of the scenario Scar had just laid out. Making Parker regret his actions would make me feel better, and a free dinner never hurt anyone. Except in that episode of Family Guy based on *And Then There Were None,* but as a rule, it didn't. 'Fine, you've twisted my arm.'

Scar used the sofa as support and jumped up into the air in excitement. On landing, she started clapping her hands, and showing way too much enthusiasm. Curiouser and curiouser.

'So you like Jackson then?' I asked, coming to the only conclusion that would really make sense. The only reason she would be pushing this, *and me,* so hard.

'I don't know,' she said, her smile etched on face and not moving anywhere anytime soon. 'But he said he wanted to talk about helping me land a big role that's auditioning next month, and I can't walk away from that kind of opportunity.'

The thing was, I agreed with her. She couldn't turn down his help, not when becoming a famous award-winning actress had been Scar's dream practically her entire life.

'I get it,' I told her, because I did. I wanted her to succeed more than anybody, and knowing how hard she'd worked and all the effort she'd put in, I couldn't hinder that because I hated Parker Daniels. 'But if it's awful, we leave, okay?'

'Okay! So, what you gonna wear?'

'I mean, let me at least get my head around the fact that we're even going first before you start giving me anxiety over my outfit. Most of my clothes are still in boxes.'

'Do you actually plan to have those unpacked anytime soon?' she asked me, crossing her arms and giving me her best parental judgey face. It was the face my mother had pulled many times in my former years, and it still gave me the chills. Even Scar's imitation was making me paranoid that Mum was going to appear out of nowhere, or knock on the door and swan inside to judge my life choices.

'Define anytime soon,' I said, half joking, and then chuckled when I saw her face fall. Scar was the clean to my chaos, and she hated having the place look so untidy. I always argued that I wasn't a dirty person, and I'd never live in filth, but I did have a habit of letting clothes pile up on the floor, as I could never be bothered to find a hanger for them. It was such an effort to hang clothes up when chances were they'd be worn again within the week, anyway.

'Whatever,' she grumbled. 'It'll be casual, right? It's only dinner at their place, and only the four of us will be eating. Won't be real fancy, will it?'

'I doubt it,' I said, thinking about what I knew of Parker. Not knowing a thing about Jackson, I couldn't tell whether he would be the type to be formal for dinner or not, but if he lived with Parker, then I assumed he was a pretty laid-back guy. Parker sure was.

'True. Right, well, I'm going to freshen up! Go, get ready.' Scar shooed me out of the living area, making it clear that I was to head directly to my room and start making myself look somewhat presentable.

'Sir, yes, sir.' I saluted her, and she rolled her eyes at me good-naturedly. Scar had always been the bossy one of the two of us, keeping me in line whenever a school project needed doing, or we needed to be on time for some meeting.

'Shut it, Allman,' she said with a laugh, and we parted ways in the hall, each entering our own rooms.

Now, what to wear?

I SHUFFLED, uncomfortable in my own skin, as I kept having to stop myself from fidgeting with the skirt of my dress and tights.

Once again, Scar looked like a bombshell pin-up model, and I looked like her dumpy sidekick who had never understood how to dress to accentuate what your mama gave you. Not that my mother had given me these curves; my mum was tall and sinewy, and she *never* had trouble finding clothes that made her look wonderful. I'd always been jealous of that.

'Stop fixing your tights, you look amazing.'

Scar and I were standing outside the door of the boys' apartment, and all I could think was that it was nowhere near as grand as I'd expected it to be. The door itself was nondescript, and really rather plain. Just a regular front door of a relatively regular apartment. I didn't know why, but I'd got it in my head that they would be living in a penthouse suite in one of the city's highest skyscrapers, looking out over the skyline and surveying their kingdom. But in actuality, the building had been upscale, yes, but not like some of the places I knew existed around here.

'Not as impressive as I thought it would be,' I told her, needing to voice my thoughts, hoping she'd agree with me. Scar shrugged, and knocked on the door using the large, polished silver character knocker that was in the shape of a snail. Nice to see that the two of them had a sense of humour.

The door swung wide open to reveal Jackson standing on the other side, dressed casually in a tight black shirt and jeans.

'Come in,' he said, gesturing for us to enter. We did so and removed our coats. Jackson hung them on a coat rack by the door. The hallway was large and spacious—maybe this flat was more like the Tardis than it seemed at first glance.

'Radley, no!' Parker called from further in the flat, and I didn't have a moment to wonder what on earth he meant before a ginormous brown dog came bounding up to the two of us, his tail wagging in excitement.

Before I could move, the dog jumped up onto his hind legs and placed his paws on my shoulders, causing me to stumble backwards slightly. Wow, this dog had some strength.

'Down, Radley,' I said, trying to make my voice as stern as I could, using the name I'd heard Parker shout. *Radley?* Nope. Not going to think about why that would be his name. For all I knew, the dog could be Jackson's.

Parker appeared, looking worried, and a laugh bubbled out of my throat involuntarily. The worry melted away when he saw that everything was under control, Radley now sitting at my feet like a good boy. He was a boy, right?

'Is Radley a "he"?' I asked, not looking at Parker, and directing my question to the party as a whole.

'Yep,' Parker replied, coming closer now that he saw everything was under control. He crouched down to give him a stroke. And if I hadn't decided I would hate him forever, my heart would have melted a tiny bit at the interaction. 'He's only two, would you believe it?'

'I wouldn't,' Scar piped up, watching us with a frown. Telepathically, I tried to send out waves to ask her what was wrong, but she looked away to stop my eyes from looking too hard. *Interesting*.

'I'm so happy you could come, girls,' Jackson said, walking down the corridor away from us, so we'd follow. Scar instantly trailed after him, taking in her surroundings as she did so. The place was bright and clean, which surprised me a lot. Nothing about this place was fitting my assumptions, and irritation filled me, because I liked to believe that I had everything figured out and squared away neatly in a box.

Parker hadn't moved from his spot; he was watching the dog and me intently.

I scratched Radley's head, and whispered under my breath, 'You are a cutie, aren't you? Shame about your daddy.'

'I heard that,' Parker said.

I smiled widely at him and said, 'Oh, did you? My bad.'

I shrugged and stepped away from Radley.

With a bounce in my step, I made my way towards the others, following the sounds of Jackson's and Scar's voices as they were talking somewhere nearby.

'Would you like some wine, Atticus?' Jackson asked, as he handed a glass of rosé to Scar.

'I'll have what she's having, please,' I answered, smiling. He seemed nice enough, and so far, he'd been acting like a regular guy and not a famous actor. Although, not having met many famous people, I didn't have anyone to compare him to.

'So, what you cooking?' Scar asked, taking a seat on a stool at the breakfast bar. I sat on the one next to her, thanking Jackson when he handed me my glass of wine. A quick sip told me that it wasn't the four-pound bottle we usually drank at our place; this was fruity, and fresh, and overall better.

'Spinach and mascarpone tagliatelle,' Jackson replied, and I nearly fell off the stool I was sitting on.

'You what now?' I asked, clearly unable to form a coherent sentence. I *loved* that meal, and it had been one of my favourites for years. Ever since...oh, now it all made sense. Parker knew it was my favourite, and obviously he'd asked Jackson to make it specifically, to get on my good side. If anything, it made me more mad that he was trying to win me around with pasta. Pasta was sacred, and no man should ever use it for their own agenda.

'It's a recipe Parker sent me,' he said, turning back to face the stove—probably as a way to avoid my narrowed gaze. 'I love to cook.'

'That's cool,' Scar said, nursing her wine glass like a life raft. 'Atti and I rarely cook at home. We're takeaway girls all the way.'

I nodded, drinking more of the wine, wondering where Parker had got to. He still hadn't appeared from down the hall, and neither had his dog.

'I love Italian food,' I said, thinking of all of my favourites. 'Pizza and pasta are on par with sex, I'd say.'

'You sure about that?' A velvety voice asked near my ear, and I jumped into the air, spilling my wine over the side of the glass and onto my skirt. *Shoot.*

'Yes,' I said, my voice venomous. 'Very sure.'

'Shame,' Parker said, his blue eyes glistening with mischief. 'Can't say I've ever had a pizza that good.'

'You've clearly never had a stone baked one from Carlo's then,' Scar said, joining in to back me up. I gave her a smile in thanks, glad that she was here with me. *Hang on a minute.* I was only here because Scar had wanted me to be, not the other way around.

'She's not wrong,' Jackson agreed, and I warmed to him more, wondering how he'd ended up lumped with loser number one, who was hovering near the entrance to the room.

'Where's Radley?' I asked, not seeing him anywhere. There was a large crate in the living area, but that was empty except for a couple of chew toys.

'Crate in my room,' Parker said. 'It's where he goes during dinner time. Can't have him anywhere near our food, and no matter how many times I've taken him to obedience classes, he just can't seem to grasp that the food on the table isn't for him.'

We all broke out into laughter at Parker's exasperated face, and the moment I clocked what I was doing, I stopped abruptly. *I must not laugh at anything Parker Daniels says,* I told myself sternly. The room went silent, and a layer of tension appeared suddenly.

'He's cute,' I said, as a reflex, looking for something to say.

'He's a scoundrel,' Parker said.

I couldn't help myself: 'Like father, like son.'

My face probably showed my feelings on the matter, and I knew the frown covering my face was a deep one. Our eyes locked, and a slight tug of something pulled on my heart. It wasn't love, definitely not, but it also wasn't as unaffected as I wanted it to be.

'Grubs up!' Jackson said, breaking the tension between us.

I blinked, the stars disappearing from my vision, and the room coming into focus again.

Perfect timing.

Eight

Parker

DINNER TASTED AMAZING. Jackson really had outdone himself, and not for the first time, I was beyond chuffed that he was my roommate. I'd never mastered cooking anything more than instant noodles.

The conversation, however, hadn't been as amazing. If anything, it had been stilted and awkward since we moved from the kitchen to the dining table. It was as if the moment we all sat down in a more formal setting; we didn't know how to act around one another.

'So, how did you two meet?' I asked, using my fork to gesture between Scarlet and Jackson, who were sitting opposite each other. Meaning I'd been sitting opposite Atticus, which was something I wouldn't be complaining about, although I was pretty sure she'd hissed to Scar about it at first.

'On set,' Jackson answered, smiling faintly. 'Scar's great in her scene, and we met over at the food table in between takes.'

Scarlet chuckled, clearly remembering the meeting,

amused by what she saw in her mind. She'd always wanted to be an actress, and any show our school had put on, she'd played the lead role every single time.

'I was grabbing a donut, and pretending that I wasn't.' She shook her head at herself. 'Honestly, this dick shows up and tells me to just pick it up already, and move out of his way.'

'Hey!' Jackson said. 'In my defence, I'd just finished shooting an emotional scene, and I needed the sugar.'

'Yeah, yeah,' she said, twirling her pasta around her fork. 'You were hangry. Since then, I've made sure to avoid him when he's like that.'

'Totally valid,' I said, amused at Scar's accuracy. She'd nailed Jackson, and how he acted when hungry. 'He's definitely a soft-heart when not hungry though.'

'Shut up, man.' Jackson stabbed my hand with his fork, and I winced. Dickhead. Obviously, he hadn't liked being called a soft-heart. Touchy subject.

'Don't listen to him,' Atticus piped up, having just drained her third wineglass of the evening. 'This prick can't talk about being hangry, and as for the whole soft-heart thing, he's just jealous that he doesn't have one.'

She rolled her eyes and looked at me straight on, hatred blazing out of her gaze. There was no way I could just take it and say nothing in response. She didn't know me anymore, and she'd never even given me a chance back then to explain everything. My aim for the evening was to get her into a private conversation, a real one, and make sure she heard what I needed to say.

'I know Radley would beg to differ. I'm a great dog dad.' I smiled at her, a teasing one that hopefully was getting under her skin. Pretty sure I breathed earlier, and she sighed like it was the worst sound she'd ever heard. A bit dramatic, even for her.

'Poor Radley knows no different.' Atticus poured herself another glass of wine, and the amount she had already consumed was making her bold. 'He didn't get to choose you, and I'm sure if he was able to choose, he'd have picked literally anybody else.'

'Thanks for that ringing endorsement,' I bit out, frustrated, and slightly put out that she would imply my dog wouldn't want me. I'd given Radley a wonderful life, and just because she thought I was the devil incarnate, didn't mean it was true. 'Nice to know you're still bitter, Atti.'

'Bitter?' she spat with derision. 'Who are *you* calling bitter?'

'You!' I replied, exasperated. Jackson and Scar kept quiet; both of them had resumed eating, or drinking, and were averting their gazes. 'You've never let me explain.'

'Explain what? How you *cheated on me* with Alexa Cummings?' she said, raising her eyebrows at me, while her face slowly reddened in anger.

'I didn't!' I replied, trying to stay in my seat and not jump up out of frustration. She never had listened to me and had never believed the truth of that evening. From the moment she'd walked into that room, she'd only seen what she wanted to see. 'But you walked out with no goodbye before I could even get a word out.'

'I know what I saw,' she said, and drained her glass again, effectively ending the conversation. Jackson and Scar were still silently eating their food, and I knew that they were sharing looks about what had just happened.

'This food is so good,' Scar said, looking at Jackson,

trying to ease the tension that had entered the area. Sitting around this table, as a four, had been awkward from the beginning of the meal, but now it was beyond that. Atticus kept throwing evil glares at me, as if it were all my fault she felt so mad. The real kicker? Her stubbornness was part of why I'd fallen for her in the first place. Even at school, as teenagers, Atti had integrity and had made me work for it; turning me down for at least a solid year before agreeing to one date.

'Thank you,' Jackson replied modestly, as if the guy had no clue how good his cooking was. He definitely did. It was something he prided himself on. Plus, he rubbed it in every single time I burned something simple, like toast. Jackson stood up and brushed his hands on his jeans in a nervous gesture. 'Who would like dessert?'

Atticus perked up, and hearing one of her favourite words, she said, 'Dessert? Yes, please.' Then, after contemplating for a moment, she added, 'What is it?'

We all chuckled, and the dark cloud from earlier dispelled slightly through Atticus's love of anything sweet. Ever since we'd met, she'd been able to put away as much chocolate and sugary treats as a sweet store could hold, and even though I knew it made her self-conscious, I loved her for it, anyway.

'Tiramisu,' Jackson said, holding the dish up so that we could all see it. 'Thought we could continue on with the Italian theme.'

A chorus of 'Please!' erupted, all of us eager to eat the tiramisu—partly to ease the tension, and so that we all had something to do other than make awkward small talk.

I took in a deep breath, and thought, *This is it, now or never.*

'Atti,' I said, and she looked at me with a withering gaze, 'could we talk in private after dinner?'

'No,' she said, without thinking about my question, even for a second. She'd made up her mind before I'd even finished asking it. I would bet money on it.

'How comes?' I asked, baiting her a little. I wanted to know what her response would be, but one thing I did know about Atticus Allman was that the girl could hold a grudge for eternity if need be. Pretty sure she hadn't forgiven Preston Wright for destroying her Henry VIII figurine back in primary school, and that had taken place nearly twenty years ago.

'Because,' she said, her tone filled with menace, 'I don't want to.'

'Real mature, Atti,' I told her as Jackson returned to the table with bowls of tiramisu, placing them down in front of the girls first.

'I don't think you can say anything to *me* about maturity, Parker Daniels.' The anger on her face startled me. I knew the girl disliked me these days, but up until that moment, it hadn't truly clocked in my mind just *how much*. She looked up at Jackson, and her face changed completely. Her smile was wide as she beamed up at him. 'Thank you.'

'No problem,' he replied, taking his seat once again.

I knew it wasn't Jackson's fault, but I was feeling a bit jealous of how she was interacting with him. They'd barely known each other all of a minute, yet she was giving him kind eyes and wide smiles that I wanted to see aimed in my direction. I was considering getting Radley out of his crate just to make her smile; yes, I was aware of how low I'd sunk as I contemplated using my dog as a bargaining chip. I'd hit a new low.

'Why don't you hear him out?' Scar asked Atticus loud enough for Jackson and me to hear her. I smiled behind my spoon that was piled high with my dessert, hoping that she wouldn't see and fling hers at me.

'Are you serious?' Atti grit out through her teeth, and I knew how pissed she was with the question. 'You're meant to be on my side.'

Scarlet shrugged her petite shoulders, and her blonde curls bounced around her, looking like a fluffy cloud. I shook my head fast, knocking that thought away. I wasn't the kind of guy that thought of hair as a *fluffy cloud.* Being around Atticus must have messed me up more than I'd realised. I couldn't think right with her around, her vanilla scent entering my personal bubble.

'Give the boy a chance,' Scar said, looking at me. I could tell that she meant it. She may dislike me, and hate me because of what happened with Atti, but she clearly loves Atti enough to want her to be happy. Or to move on from the past. Either way, it worked in my favour. 'He's desperate.'

'Gee, thanks, Scar.' I scoffed at her statement. I wasn't *desperate*. I took a major offence at that. I just wanted to tell my truth to Atticus. 'Who invited you?'

'You did, champ.' Scarlet laughed, and I rolled my eyes at her, feeling like the child she thought I was.

'Nuh-uh,' I replied, 'Jackson did.'

'Originally,' he said, his voice low. I kicked him underneath the table, small yet hard, and he grunted in pain. 'I'm glad you could come.'

Scarlet beamed at him, and I saw Atticus look between them and then huff slightly. Clearly, like me, she could see the chemistry building between those two, and neither of us knew how to stop it. Not that we *should* stop it. Our friends deserved to get their flirt on.

'*I'm* not,' Atti said under her breath.

'Something you want to share with the class, Atti?' I asked loudly, drawing all attention at the table back to her.

'Nope,' she said, popping her 'p' with a pout. 'Not if the class includes *you*.'

'Children,' Scarlet said with a laugh, 'leave this to the playground, yeah?'

'Tell him that,' Atticus said, crossing her arms across her chest, causing my eyes to gaze downwards. She really shouldn't have done that. Especially if she didn't want me to appreciatively gaze at the cleavage I knew she was hiding underneath that plain dress. 'My eyes are up here, dickwad.'

'I'm aware,' I drawled, 'but they're not looking at me quite as nice as the rest of you is.'

Okay, I'd tried to be smooth, tried to be flattering, but I could recognise that what I'd said had made no sense. I'd been put on the spot, and even though I'd looked at her chest, knowing she would have something to say about it, I still hadn't thought up a comeback; rookie mistake.

'Right …' she trailed off, and the four of us went back to eating our dessert like nothing had happened. Really, it was a way for the four of us to disconnect from the awkward tension that had seeped into the room.

Hm. Wonder if I could put my foot in my mouth even more if I tried.

AFTER DESSERT, Jackson and Scarlet had gone to the sofas in the living area and were discussing a new script that Jackson had been given. I knew Scarlet really wanted to be a big-time actress; it had been her dream since we were young, after all.

Atticus had floated off by herself to stand on the balcony, a glass of wine gripped in her hand, as she stared across the city lights. From up here, the view was amazing. It had been one of the selling points in my eyes.

'Now or never, mate,' I whispered to Radley, hoping that he'd understand. Sometimes, with the way his eyes looked at me, I believed that maybe he had a human soul in there, trapped by a witch to live out eternity in the form of a Newfoundland. What? Crazier things had happened.

I made my way over to the balcony door, trying to slide it open silently, to not startle Atticus.

Creakkk.

I watched as Atticus jumped at least an inch off the floor in surprise and as her wine left the confines of its glass, and proceeded to cover the entire front of her dress.

Chuckling as I went, I walked over to stand beside her, as she frantically rubbed at her dress with her hands, trying to get the excess liquid off.

'Need any help?' I asked, amused at the entire scenario.

'Not from you,' she spat, looking at me with hatred in her eyes. They were bloodshot and red; the amount of alcohol she'd consumed this evening finally catching up with her appearance. 'You caused this!'

'Me?' I asked, sweeping my hands to my chest in an overly dramatic gesture, even for me. Hah, maybe Jackson needed to get me a role in his next film, 'cause clearly I could act.

'You're a terrible actor,' Atticus said, bursting my bubble before it had even fully formed. Dream-ruiner right there.

'Am not,' I said, petulant, then realised that wasn't going to be winning her over so tried a different tactic. 'How have you been?'

My tone was genuine, or at least I thought it was, but from the look on Atticus's face, maybe it hadn't entered the air the way I'd hoped it would.

'*How have I been?*' she asked, contempt clear in every single one of her features. Her eyes had narrowed, and her lips had turned down into a frown. 'Do you mean this week? Or for the last five years?'

I opened my mouth, then shut it again. This was a trick question, and whatever answer I gave in response wouldn't be the correct one.

'You wanted to talk.' She stopped rubbing at her dress and opened her arms wide. 'So talk.'

The sound of the deadbolt being moved across on the door behind us caused me to turn around just in time to see Jackson and Scarlet, waving from the other side of the glass and laughing happily.

Guess we would be having the talk I wanted after all. Thanks guys.

Perfect timing.

Nine

Atticus

Eurgh. I hate to admit it, because trust me, I was never one for violence, but Scarlet needed to fall asleep tonight with one eye open.

Maybe even with two.

Because the stunt that she and Jackson had just pulled was NOT going to fly well with me.

They had locked me out on the balcony with Parker Daniels, of all people. I knew that Scar had been hoping all night that I would hear him out, but I never thought she'd stoop this low and be in cahoots with Parker's best friend in order to make it happen.

I grunted in frustration, out loud this time as opposed to just in my head. My arms had flown up with the sound, like an exaggerated bird. My hands were itching, and all I wanted to do was put my arms across my chest, but I'd seen the way Parker's eyes had migrated earlier and I wouldn't be giving him so ripe an opportunity again.

'What's'a matter, Atti?' he asked, his tone teasing as a playful smile formed on his face. His lips were plump and relatively pouty for a guy, but seductive all the same. No wonder he'd made a success of himself in the modelling world; the man was a stunner.

Stunner? Wow. I sounded like my mother: 'Oh Atticus. That Parker Daniels is a right stunner these days. Did you see his photos in that magazine? Positively scandalous!'

I shivered, but not from the cold. I'd been peacefully enjoying the view of the city before I'd been so rudely interrupted. Turning away from the locked door—and the guy who made my heart flutter, even when it shouldn't—I stood back up against the railing, looking once again at the skyline. The buildings didn't look quite so tall from up here, and the people down on the pavement looked like beetles, shuffling around, heading off to wherever they were meant to be. This late in the evening, they were probably heading home, or maybe out for drinks with friends. The anonymity of the city had always excited me, and after leaving university, I knew that I wanted to move into the thick of it with Scar.

'Never thought I'd see you living in the big city,' Parker said, coming closer to stand beside me at the railing.

'There are a lot of things that have changed about me,' I replied tersely, not wanting to go into further detail, but knowing that I would if he asked. I hated my reaction to him; my natural reaction, one I couldn't control. Goosebumps appeared on my arms, and a tingle travelled from my head down my spine, multiplying and making its way to all of my nerve endings. The slightly smirking smile on Parker's face caused my nipples to peak, and at that moment, I hated myself. But mostly, I hated him. How dare he make me feel this way after what he'd done? I stepped away from the railing slightly and turned to face him, my face making my displeasure clear.

Parker turned too, and matched my power stance, his legs apart, and I had to keep my eyes on his.

'I can see that,' he said, not feeling the need to keep eye contact, appraising my body from head to toe. It wasn't the first time this evening, but this was the most blatant he'd been, and I knew I should put an end to it.

'Will you stop that?' I snapped. 'Look at my face, you perv.'

He scoffed, his eyes wide, and said, 'I am not a perv!' Then, needing to defend himself further, he added, 'I can't help it if I find you attractive.'

I groaned, not wanting him to continue down this path.

'Give over,' I said. 'You do not.'

'I do too!' he said back, reminding me of a child; or a pantomime player who can't agree with the audience at any cost. 'I've always found you attractive.'

'Yeah, sure,' I told him, no longer able to prevent my arms from crossing against my chest. I tried not to push the girls up too much, though. 'You found me real attractive when I caught you slobbering all over Alexa.'

'Atti,'—his eyes were earnest, and filled with an emotion I couldn't quite place—'you've got that night all wrong.'

'How?' I spat defensively. I'd had too much to drink, and my insides were probably more wine than organs right now.

'None of what you think you saw happened.'

'So, I didn't see you kissing her when I arrived at that party?'

I tapped my toe on the floor at a rapid pace, irritated that he was making me question my own judgement; my own memories.

'You did,' he groaned out and rubbed his face, 'but it didn't happen the way you think it did.'

'And how do I think it happened, Parker?'

'Honestly? I think you think that I had intended to go to that party and cheat on you. Or that I'd taken Alexa with me as my date, or something along those lines.' Parker looked stressed at having to say the words. He was pretty bang on—I wasn't going to tell him that—but that was what I thought had happened. He'd never told me otherwise, or if he had tried to, I hadn't wanted to hear it.

'I came to surprise you,' I said, trying to keep my lower lip from quivering. 'I'd shown up at your flat, and Rooney had told me where to find you.'

'I always wondered how you'd found me,' he muttered.

'Rooney did nothing wrong,' I said, remembering the IT whiz kid that had lived with Parker during that time. The two of them had never been friends as Rooney didn't like to party, and he'd been stuck in a flat share with five lads who did want to party—Parker included. 'He was helping me.'

'That little prick wasn't helping you for the right reasons.'

'Well, maybe if you and your mates weren't so horrid to him all the time, he wouldn't have "ratted" you out like that,' I spat, frustrated that Parker was missing the point. Regardless of who told me where he was that night, he was still there in whatever version of the story was told.

'He took a dislike to us before school even started, but that's not the point here, Atti.' Parker straightened up, and sighed like the weight of the world rested on his shoulders.

'The point is, is that you never listened to me and you're still not listening to me.'

'I am too,' I told him, mad at the implication. 'I'm listening right now, aren't I?'

'You're fighting with me is what you're doing,' he said, exasperated, as his lip quirked upward in a small smile. I wondered if he got a kick out of fighting with me. The two of us had always had a turbulent relationship. Not in a bad way, but more in a push and pull kind of way. Back then, I'd really enjoyed it. Thought it meant we were meant to be—that we'd be able to deal with the real world that had come hurtling towards us faster than we'd have liked. Sadly, that wasn't the case.

'We always fight,' I said with a shrug, causing my boobs to raise with the motion and instantly catch Parker's eye once again. That boy and boobs, really. 'Parker!'

'Sorry, sorry,' he said, smiling wide with his hands out in a placating gesture.

'So, what really happened that night?' I asked, my voice small, the wind on the balcony picking up and carrying my words away from us. When he didn't instantly jump into a story, I wondered if he'd even heard me, but then he opened his mouth.

'There isn't actually that much to tell,' he said, weighing me up with a critical squint, probably not knowing where to begin. Or maybe, not knowing how to spin the tale in his favour. A large part of me still believed that I'd seen the truth. That he had cheated on me with Alexa, and the anger I'd been holding onto since was valid and justified.

'If there isn't much to say, then it won't take you long at all.'

I went to drink more out of my glass, just for something to do really, but found it empty.

Oh, yeah. I remembered now. It all went flying at my dress when Parker had startled me out here. Even more reasons to hate his existence.

'Okay, so here goes,' he said, shuffling his feet and looking to the ground. When his head raised and his eyes locked with mine, I saw a vulnerability there that knocked me back. I hadn't expected his baby blues to expose the emotions that were warring inside. My gut twisted, just a little, and all I wanted was to hear his version of what happened five years ago. The pain had never subsided for me, and the fact I was even letting him talk to me was something I wouldn't have imagined, even yesterday.

'Go on,' I told him, finally uncurling my arms from across my chest, trying to not look so defensive.

'Okay. So, here goes. Me and the guys in the flat were invited to that warehouse party and decided to go. You weren't meant to be visiting until the weekend after, and you'd texted me to say that you were going to bed early and to not message you more. Otherwise, I would have told you I was heading out.'

'Hmm,' I said, wanting him to continue but also wanting to make my scepticism audible.

'You know I would have,' he implored, reaching out and grabbing my arm, his grip gentle yet firm. 'We went to the warehouse, had a few drinks, you know how it is. Music was blaring, and loads of other uni students were there, too, but I promise you I had no intention of looking at anybody but you.'

'Just because you didn't have the intention doesn't mean it

didn't happen,' I told him, before he could get another word out.

'Atti, you clearly don't know how much I love you.' Parker's tone was soft, and if I wasn't trying so hard to stay mad, I would have swooned at his words.

'Loved me?' I queried, confused that he'd spoken in present tense.

'No. Love you,' he emphasised. 'Atti, I loved you so much then, and I never stopped. Seeing you at the wrap party. It reignited all those old feelings, and ever since learning you were coming for dinner tonight, I've been thrilled at having the chance to clear the past up with you.'

'Oh,' I said, shocked and frozen to the spot.

The glass door slid open, and I saw Scar standing on the other side, reaching out with a wine glass in her hand.

'Think the two of you have had long enough,' she said, as I grabbed the wine from her and gulped it down. Anything to prevent me from replying to Parker's words. Scarlet's arrival had been at the perfect time, and had she come a moment later, she most likely would have found me melted into a puddle on the ground at his feet.

My feet started moving towards the safety of the flat, but Parker stopped me with his next sentence.

'I'm sorry, Atticus. Please, can I have your number? I want to take you to dinner. This conversation isn't over.'

'I'm not ready for dinner,' I told him, 'but I'll get Scar to text Jackson my number.'

He nodded, knowing that I wasn't going to give him any more than that. Even agreeing to give him my number was a huge step, seeing as I'd never given him the chance to tell me his truth before. I wanted to hear the end of his story, though.

Nothing had been cleared up, and as much as I still felt all the hurt from back then, I also felt a slight bit of excitement. Like maybe I'd been holding onto my anger for too long; potentially for no reason at all.

It would take some time for my pride to come to terms with that fact.

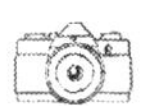

OVER THE NEXT WEEK, Parker texted me every day.

Nothing about that night, or what really happened between him and Alexa, but after hearing the sincerity in his voice and looking into his eyes on the balcony, I'd slowly started to believe that maybe I'd had it wrong all this time.

But he was definitely trying to get me to agree to go for dinner with him. I'd be lying if I said the tiniest part of me didn't want to—it did. Yet, I couldn't marry together five years of hatred with what I now knew.

Atticus, please give me a chance to clear everything up x

How long did it take you to convince me when we were teenagers? You may be waiting a while...

I chuckled at my last message to him. When we were fifteen, it had taken a whole year of asking for me to agree to go out on a date with him. I'd thought he was playing around and making a joke of me with his mates. Turns out, he'd been genuine the whole time.

I put my phone in my pocket and made my way to the kitchen.

'Atti, are you going to give the boy a break?' Scar asked from where she was sitting on the sofa in the living room next to Jackson. The two of them had been working hard every night to perfect their audition pieces. The majority of the time they'd been here at ours, but on the odd occasion Scar had been to the boys' apartment, she'd come back with a 'Parker plea', as she called it, every single time.

'I don't know what you mean,' I said, pulling a bottle of water from the fridge in order to avoid eye contact with the two of them.

'Oh, come off it,' she said, as Jackson chuckled beside her. 'Parker has been messaging you every day since we locked you out together on the balcony.'

'I'm still not overly impressed by that, you two.' I faced them, leaning up against the breakfast bar, giving them my best unimpressed look.

'Hush up. You needed to listen to the guy, and you were never going to without a little nudge.' She shrugged.

'I might have,' I said defensively, 'eventually.'

'From what I've heard, eventually would have been in another five years or so,' Jackson piped up from his spot, and I narrowed my eyes at him.

'You, mister, may be a world famous actor, but don't think that would stop me from hurting you,' I threatened, meaning every word. Jackson, who didn't believe the threat, just laughed at me.

'Ultimately, Finch, you need to give him a chance—a real chance—to say his piece. Neither of you will be happy until it's all out in the open. Cleared up, squared away, so that you can move on and be happy.'

Scar only ever called me Finch when she meant business;

when she wanted me to not just listen to her words, but take them in, too.

'Eurgh. Are the two of you going to pester me until I agree to go to dinner with him?' I asked, knowing the answer before the question had left my lips.

'You know it,' Scar said with a cheeky smile that I wanted to wipe off her face. I pouted towards them, hoping they'd take pity on me, but knowing they wouldn't.

'Fine!' I said, dramatically standing up and throwing my arms in the air, forgetting that I was holding an open bottle of water.

Like a geyser erupting, the water entered the air and came down to land abruptly on my head.

'Aargh!' I groaned, frustrated at myself for being so theatrical all the time. Once again, my gesticulating caused a problem.

I shook my hand, the water dripping off me, and grabbed my phone from where I'd ditched it on the counter top so I could flounce off.

I couldn't make a decision right now. Not when the two of them were looking at me like that. The moment the water hit me, the two of them began to laugh like children, until I gave them the glare to end all glares. They looked like they knew what was best for me, without the background of the past. Or, at least, that was true for Jackson.

Once inside the safety and privacy of my room, I screamed against my pillow in frustration, letting out everything that I'd been keeping inside since that stupid wrap party. I wish I'd never allowed Scar to convince me to go. I was way out of my league here.

My phone vibrated in my hand, and I looked at the screen, apprehensive about the message that would greet me.

Just one dinner. Please. I swear on your life, I will tell the whole truth, and nothing but the truth.

My heart swooped on reading those words—the words he'd wooed me with since we were teens—and I felt my skin prickle with heat.

Ah, fudge biscuits!

Ten

Parker

Atticus still hadn't agreed to dinner, and I was starting to get a little frustrated about it all.

Jackson had dropped me a text when I finished a shoot earlier today about needing me to bring him an important item, so I'd headed straight to ours to grab said item and made my way to the girls' apartment. Jackson had been spending a lot of time there, practising with Scarlet, and I'd barely seen him without her. There was something going on there, I would have sworn, but Jackson was adamant that wasn't the case.

When I asked, all he'd say was, "The two of us are working on her acting. Nothing else."

With no other choice but to believe him, I left it, positive he'd come to me if anything changed.

Checking my phone to make sure I was outside the right apartment, I wondered who would open the door. It was early evening by now, so I assumed that Atticus would be home. As far as I was aware, she was about to graduate from university and hadn't yet found a job to move into next.

Of course, the chance I could catch a glimpse of her was the *real* reason I had been so quick to agree to help Jackson. Usually, the man sent somebody to get the things he needed; he had a personal assistant who had a personal assistant, but apparently, he didn't want anybody to know he was helping Scar.

I knocked on the door, loud enough to be heard over the music wafting out of the cracks.

It opened wide, and I jumped back at the sight in front of me. The person I was looking at did the same.

'Oh!' we both shouted simultaneously.

'Why do you look like that?'

'What are you doing here?' Atticus asked, at the same time I spoke. We both narrowed our eyes, wary at one another, confused how we'd ended up in this position.

Atticus's face was a bright lime green, and clumpy looking, and her long hair was wrapped around what looked like cotton strips of fabric. I laughed, as the image of Mrs Doubtfire entered my mind, you know, the scene where she shoves her face in a pie to cover up her lie.

'*I* am pampering myself,' she said, gesturing at her face in circles. 'I'll ask again, what on earth are you doing here?'

I held up the bag Jackson asked me to bring, and said, 'Jacks forgot this.'

Atticus looked confused, and I wanted to smooth away the adorable frown that had taken up residence on her face.

'But Jackson and Scar aren't here,' she said. 'I thought they were at your apartment.'

'Nope, Jackson specifically told me he was here and to

bring these items for him.' Then it clicked in my head and I chuckled darkly. Those two pesky interferers. 'Atti, we've been set up.'

'We've been what now?' she asked, her frown getting deeper. Man, even with green gloop all over her face, she still managed to look cute to me. My smile widened, and I couldn't help but laugh at her confusion.

'Set up. They've bamboozled us, knowing that you were home alone tonight and that I'd swoop to Jackson's aid in order to catch a glimpse of you and convince you to let me take you to dinner.'

'Bamboozled us?' she asked, and that was when I realised that she was wearing a short silk dressing gown tied tightly around her waist, highlighting her hourglass figure. Her legs were bare, and I couldn't take my eyes away from them. 'Parker!'

'Yes ma'am,' I replied, moving my gaze up to her eyes to find her unimpressed expression. 'You were saying?'

'Oh for the love of—get in here.' She moved out of the way, so that I could enter her flat, and I made sure I brushed against her as I did so. 'Keep walking and you'll be in the living room.'

'Okay,' I said, as I walked down the hall, taking in the framed photographs in the hallway—of Scar and Atti in various different places, and poses. A smile covered my face looking at them. I'd always loved to see Atticus happy, and these pictures showed some of her happiest times since I'd seen her last.

The living area was bigger than I'd expected, with a large corner sofa that took up a lot of the space.

'You have a great home,' I said as she joined me.

'It's Scar's,' she replied with a shrug. 'She knew I needed

somewhere to go, and she had the space, so it made sense for me to come here.'

'When did you move in?' I wracked my brain to figure out whether they'd mentioned it at dinner the other night, but I couldn't remember much. Most of the time, my eyes—and my main focus—was on Atti herself.

'Couple of weeks ago,' she said. 'You want something to drink?'

'Please. Water is good, thanks.'

She laughed as she headed to their kitchen, separated from the living room by a breakfast bar, and said, 'Still can't handle too much caffeine?'

'You know it,' I replied, my mind wandering back to our school years where I lived off of energy drinks and coffee. Not a good mix. I rubbed my face with my hand, feeling as if I'd been carved open and dissected by the look Atticus was throwing my way. 'It was only one time!'

'Yeah, but you will *never* live it down.' She walked back with a glass of water in one hand and a glass of wine in the other. 'Sit down, I guess.'

'Thanks,' I replied, sitting on the furthest end of the sofa, while Atticus took a seat on the other end. 'Sorry for interrupting your evening.'

'Those two pesky interfering insects. I told them I wanted to relax tonight, by myself, with a large pizza.'

'I can leave,' I said, watching her face closely for any slight reaction from her. I didn't really mean my words, but I would leave if Atticus told me to. I'd always do whatever she told me to.

'No,' she huffed out, 'it's fine. You're here now. May as well get this talk over with.'

'Don't sound too excited,' I deadpanned.

'If you want to stay for pizza, you can,' she told me, her face not totally matching the words coming out of her mouth. 'I ordered a lot.'

A blush rose on her cheeks, her face turning the most perfect shade of pink, and I smiled at her. Knowing Atticus's love for pizza, I wouldn't be surprised if the girl had ordered enough for a small family to enjoy. The deals always grabbed her attention and she couldn't resist buying more than needed if it meant she was 'getting a bargain.'

'Thanks,' I said, knowing when it was best to be polite and not goad her further. 'You look comfy.'

'Comfy?' she sputtered out, a tiny droplet of wine leaving her mouth that she quickly wiped away with the back of her hand. 'I wasn't expecting company, believe it or not.'

'Oh, I believe it,' I said with a chuckle, but not a mean one. I wasn't laughing at her. I'd learned the hard way once not to do that.

'So.' Atticus faced me head on, her expression turning to one of displeasure at having to have this conversation when she'd least expected it. 'Talk.'

'About?'

'You said there was more to tell me about that night. So tell me.'

'What part?'

'How did you end up on that sofa with Alexa draped over you like a bad feather boa?'

'Why on earth are you comparing Alexa to a feather boa?'

She huffed, frustrated.

'Why on earth are you asking stupid questions?' she bit out. 'A feather boa was the first thing that came to mind, okay.'

'Okay,' I said, my hands in a placating gesture. Seemed I did that a lot around Atticus. 'Anyway, as I told you before, we were at the warehouse party, drinking and having a good time. Everybody was wasted, and all I wanted was to go home and message you, but I knew you'd be asleep and I didn't want to wake you. So, I got talking to a bunch of people on the sofas to pass the time.'

'Hmm.'

'And then Alexa came up to me and started asking me about my modelling. She'd heard that I was being asked to model for some relatively big brands and told me that she wanted to be a model, too. At first, she was asking for advice. Then after a bit, the other people sitting with us were telling us how good we looked together and that we should try to find some modelling work together.'

I rubbed my hands on my knees, knowing that this was the part where Atticus had walked in, and that I *needed* to make it clear that what she believed wasn't what happened.

'So then Alexa stood up from the sofa abruptly and got into a position perched on my knee. We were joking around, pulling poses while somebody took grainy images of us on their phone. It was funny, and nobody was taking anything seriously.' I took in a deep breath, steeling myself for everything that came after. 'But then Alexa grabbed my face, and pulled my lips to hers, and grabbed onto them with a fish-hook grip. I tried to swat her away, get her off of me, and I'd nearly succeeded, but then you walked through the door, and everything went downhill.'

'You don't say,' Atticus said, her eyes narrowed.

'The moment you entered and gasped, Alexa saw an opportunity and went for my neck. Started writhing around on me as if you'd walked into something a lot worse than the truth.' I changed tack at the look of murder on her face. 'Not that the truth *isn't* bad, and I completely understand that it must have looked a lot worse. But I promise you, Atticus. I swear that at no point did I willingly kiss Alexa.'

I stopped talking and took a moment to compose myself. I thought I'd forgotten all the swirling emotions this story made me feel. Had put them to the back of my mind, unbidden, not to return. Thought I was over it all, especially as I truly had started to believe that I would never get to explain anything to Atti about it. After that night, she'd not answered any of my calls. Had blocked my number on all socials. *Poof!* My girlfriend, and the girl I loved more than anything, had disappeared.

'Parker,' Atti said, looking down at her bare legs, rather than looking at me. 'I don't know what to say.'

'Say that you believe me,' I plead. It was all I'd ever wanted. For her to believe me, and to give me a second chance.

'It's hard,' she whispered, 'because I've spent so long believing what I saw. Spent so long hating you, P.'

'I know,' I replied, my voice low and cracking. I needed her to believe me. Everything I'd said was the truth.

'I want to believe you, of course I do.' Her voice was a low hush, and I could see the torment warring in her features. Could see the pain behind her bright blue eyes, glistening in the low lighting of the room. When had it got so dark outside?

The two of us remained silent for a beat, neither one of us wanting to break the spell surrounding us.

Ding-dong.

The doorbell chime brought both of us back to the room.

'Yay,' Atticus fake cheered, her voice dull. 'Saved by the bell.'

I chuckled at her attempt at a joke. We'd spent many a day watching old reruns of *Saved By The Bell* when we were teens. It had been one of Atticus's favourite TV shows, and she especially loved the murder mystery episode. Said it was a masterpiece of 80s television; whatever that meant.

As she wandered to the door to get the pizza, I tried my best to avert my eyes from her assets. The robe she wore was very short, and all I wanted was to see all of her. My dick woke up at the sight, wanting to join the pizza party, but I couldn't let him. This was *not* the time.

Down, boy, down.

AFTER PIZZA, the two of us were sitting next to one another on the sofa, having migrated closer together while eating and loosely watching a film that was playing in the background on the large flat-screen.

'If,' Atticus started, 'if I *did* believe you, and chose to give you a second chance, what's in it for me?'

'What do you mean?' I asked, not wanting to get my hopes up.

'What do I gain?' she asked, a slight smirk playing on her full lips. 'Enlighten me.'

'You'd gain a date with the one and only Parker Daniels,' I replied with a shrug, hoping my face didn't look as excited as my insides were. My gut was swishing around, doing somersaults and all kinds of acrobatics.

'You're an egotistical pig sometimes. You know that, right?'

'I'm a model,' I told her, as if that answered her rhetorical question perfectly. 'Sort of have to believe my own hype.'

'Right, but has anybody ever told you that it's unattractive?' she asked, cutting me to the core. I turned my body so that I was facing her fully, and acted wounded by her words.

'*Moi*? Unattractive?'

'Yes. You.' Atticus said, but with the smile still playing on her lips, I knew that she was joking; at least if only a little.

'Fine. I'll be real with you,' I said, reaching out to rest my hand on her knee. Even just feeling the warmth of her leg underneath my palm caused shivers to run down my spine. For years I'd dreamed of having Atticus within touching distance, and now finally, it had come true. 'You'd gain my forever thanks, for starters.'

'And?'

'And...' I trailed off, my brain working a mile a minute to come up with something witty, or amusing, or real, that would keep her interest. That would convince her to give me that second chance I knew she was leaning towards. 'Honestly, Atti, I just want to give you the world. Please, give me the chance to do that.'

She blinked twice, her eyes shining with unshed tears. My lips turned up into an unsure smile as my heart rate picked up its pace. Slowly, I leaned forward, entering her personal bubble, as she did the same.

My lips pressed onto hers, then gently covered her mouth. The kiss started out slow, thoughtful, as the two of us found the pace we'd established all those years ago. As the kiss progressed, it became needier. More intimate. Every nip of the lips, every touch of our tongues, caused this agonising need in me to take this further.

But I couldn't.

I pulled back. Atticus's lips were swollen, and her eyes were glazed over, the glisten no longer from tears but from desire.

'Wow,' she whispered. 'That was...'

'That was perfect,' I replied, earnestly staring at her. The curved eyebrows that helped give her face such expression, her wide bright blue eyes that I wanted to melt into, her rosy cheeks that caused my dick to harden when he thought of all the ways he wanted to make that blush permanent.

Behind us, the front door of the apartment rattled and then, uninvited, Scar burst through calling, 'Honeyyyyy I'm home!'

Atticus, whose face went the reddest it could, muttered under her breath.

'Ah, fudge biscuits!'

Eleven

Atticus

After Parker had left, I cornered Scar to explain exactly what the plan had been between her and Jackson.

'And what, you just hoped that by coercing the two of us to spend time together that we would work it out?'

'Well, it worked, right?' she said, unrepentant. 'When I walked in, the two of you looked more than cosy!'

'As always, Scar, you have impeccable timing!' I said with a laugh. Of all the times during the night she could have returned, of course she came through the door the moment after he'd kissed me for the first time in years. It was how my luck went. There was no other way for it to have unfolded.

'How was I to know?' she asked, sweeping her hand to her heart. 'Jackson and I were sure the two of you would have sorted it out by then.'

'I mean, okay, I guess technically we had.' I looked Scar in the eyes and said, 'He told me his version of events that night.'

'And?' Her eyebrow quirked up, and that look told me that

she would react accordingly, however I felt about it all. For years, Scar had been by my side, hating on Parker, knowing that if I didn't want to give him a chance, then she'd agree with me.

'He said that it was all Alexa.'

'You believe him?'

'Yeah, I do,' I admitted. During Parker's explanation, my anger had drifted away; out to sea, and into the distance. I should have let him explain years ago. Should have never let my stubborn self ignore him and hate him blindly because of what I'd assumed. My parents had taught me better than that. 'The look on his face told me just as much as his words did.'

'Yeah, Parker's face has always given him away.' Scarlet chuckled, probably reminiscing about the times we'd caught Parker in a lie from his expression alone. 'So, what does it mean for the future? Did you agree to that dinner date?'

I cringed, knowing that Scar wouldn't like what I had to say next.

'Well...'

'Please tell me that you didn't,' she said, crossing her arms across her chest, her stare boring into me like a school teacher that knew you'd done wrong.

'I didn't. After you interrupted us,'—I narrowed my eyes at her—'he left pretty fast, didn't he? I told him to text me.'

'To text you?'

'Yeah. Why? Have I done something wrong?' I'd walked him to the door, and he'd given me a gentle, yet brief, kiss good-bye, with an, 'I'll be in touch.'

'No, no,' she rushed out, hearing the spiralling panic in my tone. 'I just meant that you didn't ask him to call? Or to pick you up at eight on Saturday?'

'Why would I have done that?' I asked, genuinely perplexed. Yeah, I now knew that I'd been unfair to him and should have listened to what he had to say, but at no point was I going to change my entire self to bow down to him. If he still wanted that date, he could ask.

'Atti, we do live in the twenty-first century, you know? There's no need for the guy to be the one to ask anymore.'

'I get that,' I told her, not liking that her tone was making me feel like a berated child. 'That's not how I see it, either. I just mean,'—I threw my arms into the air, dramatic as always —'oh, I don't know what I mean. I just want him to chase *me*.'

'Right, but the guys been chasing you since you fell over at the wrap party.'

'Cheers, Scar. Remind me of one of my greatest humiliations.'

'I'd say your greatest humiliation was the magazine articles with your head in Parker's crotch the next morning, actually.'

'Touché,' I replied, forgetting that had happened, but now not being able to think of anything else. Wow, I really did have a habit of embarrassing myself, didn't I?

'Are you going to text him at least?' Scar asked, and I thought about it for a moment. I'd told him to text me, and it hadn't even entered my mind that I could reach out first. Or if it had, I had batted it away as fast as it had come.

I was fully aware that I could reach out to him. Ask him to dinner. Make it clear that I wanted to hear from him, wanted to spend more time with him; and, if I was being honest with myself, wanted to kiss him again.

Even though our kiss had been brief, it had awakened so many emotions inside of me that I hadn't felt in a very long time.

Since splitting up with Parker way back when, I had only been on a couple of dates with guys I didn't care much about. Most of them had been blind dates, and after I'd been taken to a Star Trek marathon against my will, I put an end to those shenanigans pretty fast.

'Maybe,' I told her, not wanting to give a definite answer either way. 'I'm going to go shower. When I get out, the two of us are going to spend the evening watching our favourite films, eating popcorn, and not talking about Parker Daniels—at least for tonight.'

'Yeah, yeah,' she said, chuckling at me. 'Only if I get to choose the film!'

'Let me guess,' I said, raising my eyebrow at her. '*Dirty Dancing*? Or maybe *Fifty Shades*?'

'You know it!'

'Fine. Then after the film, maybe I'll drop Parker a message.'

Scar's face became smug, her mouth turning up at the corners, the joy evident. She rubbed her hands together.

'My work here is done.'

So. I caved.

Scarlet and I had stayed up until early morning, munching on popcorn and watching our comfort flicks together. It was the best ending to a turbulent evening. I'd also removed all the gunk from my face before the kiss with Parker, which was something I was super thankful for. The look on his face when I'd opened the door last night would stick with me for some time to come. Would have sworn that his eyebrows were going to disappear into his hairline if they'd gone any higher.

I'm game for dinner if you are. But don't mess this up. You've only got one shot.

Okay, so it wasn't as meaningful or heartfelt as it could have been, but I didn't want to give him too much. Didn't want to let him into my heart again before I knew whether he was worthy of it.

Eighteen-year-old me had given him everything. Her love, her time, and not least, her virginity. To me, that meant something; it still did.

I promise. I won't mess this up. How about burgers, Saturday night? I'll pick you up at yours.

I smiled at his reply. He knew that I was a sucker for burgers. Vegetarian burgers, anyway. I'd been a vegetarian since I was little, and it was something that Parker had always fully supported me on. At no point had he done what the other kids at school had done, which was to throw meat at me in the lunchroom, or try to hide slices of ham in my cheese sandwiches. As if I wouldn't notice ham in the shape of a bear's face staring up at me from my beloved cheese sandwiches.

Getting my hopes up wasn't something I wanted to do, *but* I had high hopes, regardless. Before it had all gone up in flames, Parker had known me better than anybody. Better than even Scar or my parents. He'd been my other half. The missing piece of my jagged puzzle. Yet he'd messed that all up with one decision; a decision that had cost him me.

I may have been sitting next to Scar on the sofa, and my face may have been turned towards the television, but for the whole of *Dirty Dancing,* my mind had been on everything that I'd done wrong. If I hadn't been so stubborn, if I hadn't blocked off all contact with Parker and his family, I may have learned the truth a lot earlier. Could have stopped a lot of heartache.

What was the saying?

Something about hindsight being twenty/twenty?

Well, hindsight was definitely opening up my eyes to some of my personal flaws. I'd always known I was stubborn. Always knew it was something that I should work on, but never really believing I *had* to.

You know how sometimes you believe that a personality trait, although toxic or unhealthy, is a part of you, whether it's good or not?

That was me with my stubbornness. Well, that, and a few other traits that I didn't want to put a magnifying glass to just yet.

Now I had to keep myself sane until Saturday night. Had to stop myself from repeating my past bad decisions—or at least stop the reel of them that was playing on repeat in my mind.

If we were going for burgers, I had a feeling I knew where he was taking me, which meant that I didn't need to overly dress up. Parker knew how much I hated dressing up, and once again, without even trying to, the man had shown me how much he paid attention to me and all of my little nuances.

The best place for burgers in this city was Carillo's. The place was a mix between a bar and a fast-food restaurant and the walls were adorned with rock n roll memorabilia from years past. I loved going there and taking in the guitars and the outlandish costumes everywhere you looked. I always hoped we'd get seated in a different booth, so that I could look at something new.

I wasn't even that into rock 'n' roll music, I just enjoyed history, in any way, shape or form. It was one of the reasons why I'd studied it at university, after all. That, and my love of Henry VIII and the 1920s.

What time should I be ready for?

How about eight? Leaves us time to bowl before eating.

It was official.

Parker Daniels had once again stolen my heart.

Like a thief in the night. Like a robber in those cartoons who are stereotypical and outlandish. Like every other cliché that existed out there.

And I didn't know how I was meant to compete with that. How was I meant to not fall, now that he held my heart in his large hands?

Saturday came, and I'd put on a comfortable pair of skinny jeans and a floating top that showed off some cleavage, but not enough that people would get an eyeful while I bowled.

'Are you excited?' Scar asked, watching me stress out, rushing around the apartment throwing things in my bag.

'Err,' I replied, unsure how to answer her.

Was I excited? Kind of.

Ever since I'd agreed to go for this dinner, Parker and I had been texting constantly. Some days it was a full in-depth conversation, discussing things in each other's past that we'd missed out on. Then on others, he would send me a silly video or a cute picture of Radley after a bath.

My heart wanted him. Of course it did. But my head hadn't fully caught up with my heart. Or it was being more sensible, at least.

'He's taking you to your favourite place. And he's taking you bowling!' Scar squeals, as if Parker was taking me to the Ritz or something.

'I'm aware,' I deadpanned in response. 'Doesn't change the past though, does it?'

'Well...no. But he's already told you that you had it all wrong.'

The door chime rang through our flat, and my stomach dropped. *Shit.* It was only seven. Surely he wouldn't have arrived an entire hour early? He knew that I wasn't the best at time management.

Scar went to the door and opened it to find Parker standing on the other side. His hair was perfectly styled in a way that made it seem as if he hadn't styled it at all, but I knew his secrets. He'd probably spent at least half an hour on it, minimum.

He wore black jeans, a white T-shirt and a black leather jacket.

Damn. He looked mighty fine.

It always amazed me how something so simple could look so impressive on him. Ever since we were fourteen, he'd had a certain swagger that no other guy I'd met before, or after, could compete with. And if I was being honest with myself? I'd never really tried hard enough to look elsewhere.

'Hey Scar,' he said, holding a stuffed teddy tight in his grip. His eyes found mine, and his face softened. The smile that covered my face was an involuntary reaction. 'Hey you.'

'Hey yourself,' I murmured, feeling shy all of a sudden, which was ridiculous. This guy had seen me embarrass myself more than any other, so why my cheeks were turning red in that moment I couldn't be sure.

He entered the room and came straight to where I was standing.

'You're an hour early,' I reprimanded, crossing my arms and giving him the evil eye.

'I couldn't wait to see you. Had to make sure you didn't bail on me,' he said with a small grin, showing off those dimples in his cheeks that always made me swoon.

'Smooth,' Scar whispered, laughing at us both.

'This is for you,' Parker said, drawing my attention back to him, pushing the teddy forward for me to take. It was fluffy and white, holding a tiny, bear-sized bouquet of flowers. I giggled, warmth spreading through me at the gesture.

I hated receiving flowers as a rule, and had never wanted to be given them by Parker. Give me chocolate or cheese any day of the week over flowers. So he had come up with a way to give them to me without me getting mad about it. Like this bear, over the years he had arranged small gifts that incorporated flowers, but not overly, and not enough for me to get annoyed by. Basically, if I didn't have to keep them alive, or put effort into it, then I was happy.

'Thank you,' I gushed, inspecting the tiny shirt, waistcoat and trousers the bear was wearing. He looked dapper, and I knew that Parker had gone to one of those stores where you pick the bear and the outfit out yourself. I rolled my eyes at his childish antics, but secretly loving them all the same.

'Want to know his name?' he asked, his blue eyes searing me.

'Do I?' I asked, wondering whether I wanted to know. Parker had been proving in the short two-week period that we'd been back in one another's lives that he still remembered a lot about our time together. Still remembered a lot about *me*.

'It's Henry,' he said, a slight tilt of his lips accompanying the words. As the name left his mouth, I gasped a little; the tiniest intake of audible breath, letting him know what that meant to me.

'Aww,' Scar said, bringing me back to the moment. I'd totally forgotten that there was a witness to this.

Scar obviously remembered the significance of the name, too.

Henry was the name that a young, wide-eyed Atticus and Parker had decided on for their first son. We were hopeful that we'd found our forever, and had talked about marriage and children on more than one occasion. But the name meant a lot to me for more than that reason:

One, it was the name of Henry VIII, and we all knew how I felt about him.

Then two, it was my grandfather's name. He had passed away back when Parker and I had first started dating, and it had hit me hard.

'Thank you,' I said, meaning every syllable. 'Ready to head out?'

'Ready if you are.'

Twelve

Parker

ATTICUS LOOKED AMAZING.

Honest to God, amazing. Everything about her was so effortless; yet I knew she'd have stressed for hours about her appearance. She had never been able to see herself the way I did. The way anybody else saw her.

'So, bowling first?' she asked when we reached the hub of the city centre. The city was alive with people, and noise filled the night sky. I loved the excitement; loved busy areas filled with people. Lucky that I did, seeing as being a model meant that I dealt with a lot of crowds.

'Of course, bowling first,' I said with a smile. 'You hate bowling on a full stomach. Means you don't score as many strikes.'

'You remembered.' She beamed at me, her bright teeth all showing, and I felt a nervous buzz of energy settle in my stomach.

'Course I remembered.' I smiled tentatively at her. I was

beyond thrilled that she had come out on a date with me. Had taken a chance to give *me* a second chance.

'Well, what are we waiting for, then?' she asked, picking up her pace to head towards *Lakeland Lanes*. It wasn't the newest, or the flashiest, bowling alley around, but it was where we had always headed ever since we were teenagers. This was where we'd had our first date. The place where we'd shared a lot of memories, actually.

'Hey, wait up!' I called after her, watching the back of her head as it bobbed through the crowd towards the entrance. 'Atti!'

'Catch up, loser.' She stopped at the doors and turned to wait for me. The smile was still plastered on her face, and her cheeks were flushed from the power walk she'd just completed.

'I'm here, I'm here,' I said as I reached out to take her hand in mine.

The two of us headed into the bowling alley hand-in-hand and it felt right. Like everything in life was slotting back into the correct slots.

On reaching the circular desk, I said, 'Lane for Parker.'

The teenager behind the desk popped their gum and looked unimpressed. Until she realised who I was. Then her face lit up and her entire demeanour changed.

'You're Parker Daniels,' she whispered. I heard Atticus scoff next to me, and I gripped her hand tighter in warning.

'Nope,' I told her, 'just look like him, I guess.' I shrugged, hoping my cavalier attitude about it all would throw her off the scent.

'Sure,' she said sceptically, raising her eyebrow at me in question. 'Course not.'

Her eyes glinted with excitement, and I was sure she hadn't believed me. *Great.* How fast would it take her to alert all of her friends?

'Could I speak to the manager?' I asked, trying to take a hold of the situation before it could escalate.

'Of course,' she said. 'Three games, yeah?'

'Yep,' Atticus piped up. I knew I'd done the right thing by booking in for three games. Atticus was competitive, and I knew that she would turn this into a tournament of sorts.

'Head over to the counter to grab your shoes,' the teenager gestured to the desk over in the corner. 'I'll have the manager come over when he can.'

'Thank you,' I said. I hoped that my politeness would stop her from putting the news out on her social media for everybody to see.

It really wouldn't make a great impression on Atticus if we were mobbed at a bowling alley on our first date back together.

'Come on, famous model boy,' Atticus joked over her shoulder as she headed to grab her shoes. There were lanes these days where you could wear your own shoes, but I knew Atticus wouldn't have appreciated me booking one of them.

She loved putting on the shoes. Loved feeling like she meant business, and that she was a highly skilled bowler. Atticus's enthusiasm always made me smile. She wasn't enthusiastic about a lot of things, but when she was, you could feel it in your bones. The excitement was palpable in the surrounding air. It always made me happy to see her happy.

'I hope you've been practising over the years,' she said, coming to stand in front of me while I tied my shoelaces. I looked up, taking her all in with my eyes as I did so, perusing every inch of her tight jeans that hugged every curve.

'You know me,' I said, 'been hanging around in bowling alleys every weekend since I moved back here on the off chance I'd see you.'

'Ha,' she mocked. I loved this side of her. The joking, carefree Atticus that she became around me. The one I wanted to keep close to my chest and never let anybody have ever again.

We hadn't had that conversation yet.

The one where we opened up about any partners we'd had in the time apart, but I was happy to tell her everything. I was an open book where Atticus was concerned. Always had been; she'd just never given me the time or chance to tell her the truth when it had mattered.

After I had a brief conversation with the manager, ensuring our privacy while we were here, we made our way to our lane—number thirteen—and it felt like destiny. This was the lane we'd played on back in the old days. Atticus believed that the number thirteen had just got a bad rep from those who 'misunderstood it.'

'My lucky number!' Atticus looked at me, crossing her arms across her ample chest with a face full of glee. 'You're going down, model boy.'

'We'll see about that, princess.'

'How ON EARTH did you manage to get three strikes in a row?' I called, while Atticus made her way back from the lane to the seating area.

Without looking in my direction, Atticus picked up her glass of Diet Coke and held it, smirking, up at the scoreboard that had updated with her new score.

She took a deep draw from her straw and swallowed. The way she was so focused on her task had my 'friend' stirring to half-attention. He wanted to be the straw, and I couldn't blame him. Atticus's lips were a perfect pout and my memory already had the visuals it needed for this to become uncomfortable for me real fast.

'Take that, loser,' she said, placing her drink back down on the table, the smile on her face small, but her eyes were shining with amusement. She was enjoying this, and by this, I meant me losing, big-time. Atticus had pulled three strikes out of the bag in a row, and I'd been lucky to even hit five pins down at a time.

I'd wanted to play with the barriers up, but nooooo, apparently that was blasphemous. It was cheating according to Atti, and we weren't going to live our lives that way.

So here I was, Mr Gutterball, making a right fool out of myself all while hoping I was impressing Atticus just a little bit.

Not sure who I was kidding, though.

'Not my fault my ball's got a magnet in it drawing it to the sides.'

'Oh, sure. Nothing to do with that wonky bowl you have.'

'What're you saying about my wonky bowl?' I asked, pretending to be outraged. I'd missed this. Missed her. The banter and the fun times. It was nice to see her face now, happy and bright, and not the memory I had of her with mascara streaks running down her cheeks and her eyes red-rimmed with pain.

'Well, it's not great, is it?' She chuckled, and I found myself joining her. I couldn't help it; even if it was at my expense.

'I always try to overcorrect it,' I told her, loving the way she bit her bottom lip to stop the snorting and giggles.

'Well, this is your last bowl, so make it count,' she said, still holding in her laugh.

I went up to the ball return and picked up the size ten I'd been using all game, then placed it back down. Desperate times called for desperate measures. Picking up the bright pink size six, I smiled brightly as I stuffed my large fingers inside the tiny holes.

'That ball is way too small for you,' Atticus called over, this time letting her laughter free. 'You'll end up taking somebody's eye out when it flings off your fingers backwards!'

'Never!' I called back, not taking my eyes off of the pins in front of me at the end of the lane. I lifted the ball close to my lips and whispered, 'Daniels' magic. Daniels' magic.'

I coughed, so nobody could hear me, but it was something me and my family had done for years. You know how everybody seems to have that crazy aunt who wasn't really their aunt but their mother's best friend? Well, mine was Auntie Carol. She'd been Mum's best friend since they met at work in their early twenties, and my entire childhood was filled with stories she'd told. Crazy stories. Gross stories. And one of the things she did often was whisper to her dice during a game of Monopoly or Cluedo. Obviously, she said her surname and not mine, but it was something that stuck ever since. My sisters and I still did it when playing board games together at Christmas time.

'Stop talking to your ball and throw it!' Atticus shouted from the seating area, and I could hear the amusement in her tone. She was getting a kick out of how poor I was doing. She'd always been competitive, and I definitely wasn't giving her much of a fight.

'Yeah, yeah.'

I stepped up to the line and bowled the ball, praying it would leave my fingers in the direction of the pins.

When it did so, Atticus and I both cheered and clapped.

Then I heard the most perfect noise.

One by one, each pin clattered to the lane, each one a musical note I was happy to hear.

'As if!' Atti sputtered, and I turned to face her, a broad smile covering my face.

'Strrrrrrrrrike!' I called out in my best sports commentator voice. 'He shoots. He scores.'

'And he still loses,' Atticus said with a giggle. 'You can't even call it a strike, P. It was the second chance of the frame!'

'Well, I'm still mighty impressed with my bowling skills, A.'

She shoved my shoulder, causing my step to falter, and I had to catch myself before I landed on the slippery surface. These bowling shoes were lethal.

'Come on, model boy,' she said, holding out her arm to steady me. 'Let's go get burgers. I'm starved.'

'Your wish is my command, fair lady.'

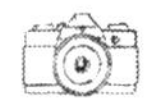

CARILLO'S WAS our favourite burger joint. Had been since it opened. And I knew that I was pulling out the big guns by bringing her here. She knew it too.

'I hope they still have that Green Piece burger,' Atticus said as we walked up to the bright red sign of the restaurant. 'I've been craving it ever since you said burgers.'

'Reckon they do, and if not, I'm sure we can ask Chef

Carillo to make it for you. You know he's always had a soft spot for you.'

'Oh, shh. He hasn't. He just liked my formal dress that time we came here after the dance. Which now that I think about it, is a little suspect.'

We both laughed. That dress had been pretty amazing, even if all I could remember about it was that it was tight and red.

'You looked beautiful that night.' I looked her over from head to toe. 'You look beautiful tonight, too. Did I already mention that?'

'No,' she said with a shy smile. 'Not yet.'

'Well, you do.' I reached out my hand to take hers and tug her towards me so that we could walk the last few steps with my arm around her shoulder. 'You always do.'

The blush that covered her cheeks was a light shade of red, and it instantly made me think of the times I'd seen her face flush for a whole other reason.

I coughed to cover up my wayward thoughts.

'Parker! Parker!' Voices started calling from all around us the closer we got to the restaurant.

Oops.

Maybe it hadn't been the best idea to bring her to Carillo's after all.

'Over here!'

'Who's the girl?'

'Where's Alexa?'

'Pose for a picture!'

The calls were unrelenting, and with each passing second, it felt as if more paps were appearing and crawling their way out of the nearest sewer. Because that's where most of them belonged. Among the rats.

Atticus's face was bewildered and confused. She didn't like being accosted this way—let's be honest, nobody did—and I should have thought ahead and asked Chef Carillo if we could enter through the back entrance.

I grabbed Atticus's hand and pulled her inside the restaurant, making sure to shield her with my body so that the men and their large cameras couldn't get any closer to her than they already had been.

'Is it always like this?' she asked, her voice small and childlike. The slight hesitancy in her eyes made my heart beat at an unnatural rate. I should have explained; should have given her more of a heads up. But I'd been so excited to relive our youth, I hadn't thought about it. Of course the paparazzi would be here. I came here to eat every Saturday night, usually with Jackson in tow, so the cameras knew they'd snap a decent picture if they staked the place out.

'Not always,' I said, hearing the lie in my voice the moment I said it. 'But every so often.'

'Oh.' She shook her head, and I just knew she was frustrated. This hadn't been a part of her life before, and it took some adjustment. I remembered the first time I got accosted, and it definitely took me by surprise at first. Atticus reached out her hand to pause me from making my way further into the restaurant.

'You ready for dinner?' I asked, looking past her shoulder to wave at Chef Carillo, who was gesturing at a booth table near the back he'd secured for us.

'Ready if you are,' she said, a small and uncertain smile on her face.

Thirteen

Atticus

Now that I was back at my place, with Parker beside me as we crossed the threshold, I wasn't sure what to think anymore.

A couple of weeks ago, if you'd told me I'd be in this position, I would've laughed in your face. Because absolutely zero part of me believed I would ever give Parker Daniels a second chance.

Yet here I was, doing just that.

'You want a drink or anything?' I asked, for some reason instantly turning into the hostess with the mostest.

'No,' he said, his tone low and seductive. His dark hair was slightly ruffled from the way he'd been running his fingers through it all evening, and it made him look even more delicious than usual. And believe me, the guy knew he was attractive. He hadn't become a model because he was modest.

He made a step towards me, and I backed up until my legs hit the edge of the sofa. I stumbled slightly, nearly falling backwards, but Parker saved me before I did.

'I want you,' he drawled, crowding my space so that I couldn't move. Couldn't get away even if I wanted to—and if I'm honest, I didn't want to. 'It's been too long.'

Seeing as the two of us had split when we were twenty-one, we hadn't had much of a chance to grow together sexually.

We'd lost our virginities to one another, and over the years we were together we'd had an active sex life, but it was cut short, really. We'd never got to explore one another as adults.

And man, Parker's body was now *all man*.

'Fuck, Parker, you look so good,' I growled, my tone husky and low.

'Oh, yeah?' he asked, grabbing around my waist to grab my bum cheekily. 'You're pretty sexy yourself.'

As if moved by a sense of urgency, Parker's mouth covered mine with hunger, forcing my lips open with his tongue.

The kiss was surprisingly tender and gentle, yet I knew the fire he was holding back.

His lips travelled down my neck until he kissed my pulse that thrummed in the hollow of my throat. My body was covered in goosebumps, the shiver travelling down my spine from his touch.

'Let's go to your room,' he whispered between kisses and I nodded, grabbing his hand in mine to lead him there.

'Welcome to my crib,' I joked as we entered the room. Having him in my space was strange, yet it felt so right.

'Strip,' he demanded the moment he closed the bedroom door behind him. The room was barely lit; the only light was coming in from the streetlight outside the window and it gave everything an illicit, seductive air.

Slowly, I lifted my dress up until it was over my hips,

showing off my black lace thong. I heard Parker hiss, the sound like music to my ears, giving me the courage to continue. It had been some time since he'd seen me naked, and I was a little bigger now than back then.

Once the dress was off completely, I threw it into the corner of the room, where it landed on top of the pile that was already there.

He smiled, and said, 'Nice to see some things haven't changed about you.'

I wasn't sure if he was talking about my body, or the pile of clothes in the corner. Not like I was going to find out at that moment, though.

'Atti, you look stunning,' he whispered, his gaze dropping from my eyes to my shoulders to my breasts. 'Black lace really suits you.'

'Thanks,' I mumbled, feeling a tad self-conscious and fighting my brain to stop my arms from covering myself. 'It's your turn.'

I pointed at his clothes, making it clear what I wanted of him.

In that sexy move that all hot guys seemed to have practised in the mirror to perfection, Parker took his T-shirt off over his head with one hand, then moved onto the button at the top of his jeans. His abs were defined, his tan skin enticing me in. He'd definitely worked on them a lot over the last few years. It made sense, him being a model and all.

He pulled his boxers down to reveal his impressive arousal, and my mouth watered a little.

'You like what you see?' he teased, and I nodded, gulping loudly.

With a chuckle at my expense, Parker stepped towards me,

and manoeuvred us so that we were laying down on the bed; my back on the mattress while he held himself up over me.

'You're beautiful like this,' he whispered, his hand gently fondling my breast over the top of the lace, making my nipple hard. He kissed a trail down my body and up again. Slowly, he removed my bra, taking his time to look at me. Once removed, he threw it to the floor and took one of my sensitive nipples into his mouth, nipping and licking at the small bud.

I went to grasp his hard dick in my hand, but he grabbed my wrist before I could and placed it above my head.

'This is going to be quicker than I'd like,' he admitted, his tone sheepish and unsure. 'I want to worship you all night, but this first time, I'm going to be like a teenager all over again.'

'I get it,' I whispered back, using my free hand to grip his arse, trying to move him closer to where we both wanted him most.

'Shit,' he said, capturing my eyes with his, 'do you have a condom?'

'No,' I replied, watching as his eyes seemed to lose a little of their light. 'But, if you're clean, then so am I.'

'I get checked regularly. Are you sure?'

'Don't you believe me?' I asked, a little hurt that he would think I'd lie to him about something so important.

'No, A. It's not that,' he whispered, gripping my wrist above my head still, squeezing enough to bruise. 'I just wanted to make sure this is what you want.'

'P,'—I tried to convey the full extent of my emotions in my gaze—'this is all I've ever wanted. I'm on the pill, and I haven't slept with anybody since you.'

My body flushed with embarrassment, knowing that he hadn't done the same. I didn't hold it against him, and it wasn't as if I'd actively *not* slept with somebody else. I just hadn't found the right person to give myself to since.

'You're my world, A,' he breathed out, my skin prickling with the heat of his breath.

I wanted to get off the topic and the only way I could think to do that was to distract him with myself.

Raising my legs high onto his hips, I could feel the tip of his cock nudging me, the heat radiating between us.

In one slow, delicious moment, Parker pushed inside of me, my walls clenching around him tightly. Our eyes locked, his hazelnut eyes searing mine, a hint of devilishness shining out at me.

Once he was fully seated, Parker began to move, building up speed, and a moan of ecstasy slipped from my lips. I couldn't control it. Parker had the power to ignite me from the inside out, the electricity snapping between us scorching through my entire body.

If I thought about it, maybe I had had been waiting for this moment. For Parker to be in my arms, and my bed, again. Our time together was cut short by my actions, and this, this felt like redemption for us both.

He bit my neck gently, and I moaned louder. My pulse was thrumming away, my heart feeling as if it was about to leave the confines of my chest. The raw emotion between us was palpable in the air, and all I could think about was how much I love Parker. Not *loved* like I originally thought, but *love*.

As Parker picked up the pace, my stomach fluttered with a million butterflies, my wrist still held above my head, while my other hand gripped him, pulling him deeper into me. He was hitting the spot inside that caused pleasure to flush through me.

My orgasm moved through me, curling my toes as I clenched my thighs, holding him in place while I fell apart underneath him.

With one last push, Parker emptied himself, a soft moan leaving his mouth against my ear.

'You're mine again, A.'

In my head, I thought of the words I wished to whisper, but couldn't bring myself to in case I ruined the moment. In case I'd got this all wrong.

I love you, P.

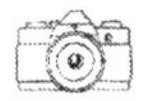

WAKING up beside Parker just felt right.

My heart soared at the sight of him, his face peaceful as he feigned sleep. I knew he was awake, though. A lot may have changed over the years, but that was one thing that hadn't. Parker had always made it a habit to pretend to be asleep. As teenagers, it usually meant that he got out of cleaning up in the morning after house parties.

'I know you're awake,' I whispered as I leaned in to kiss his cheek, my breath fanning across his face and causing goose-bumps to prickle on his arm.

'Stop talking and kiss me, woman,' he replied, moving his arm to wrap it around me and pull me closer. Parker turned his head to kiss me full on the lips, an exaggerated noise as he did so. 'So, I've got a question to ask you.'

'You do?' I leaned back and raised one singular eyebrow at

him, wondering what on earth could come out of his mouth next.

'Yep,' he said with a smile. 'My family's having a garden party barbeque today and I'd love it if you came with me. I know Mum and Dad have missed you, and you've always been on good terms with Cass and Zara.'

'Right...'

'So, will you come with?' He looked so sincere, so endearing, that I knew I wouldn't be able to say no, no matter how much I may have wanted to.

'I don't know ... it's been a long time since I saw your family, P. What if they don't want to see me?'

'My parents love you, Atti. They've reprimanded me so many times about how I shouldn't have ever let you go. Believe me, they'll be chuffed.'

'Only if you're sure?' I pulled the duvet up to cover myself, feeling strangely vulnerable lying here naked with him, now that we were on the subject of his family.

I'd always felt uncomfortable seeing them around town; which was something that had happened more times than I could count on my two hands. I guessed that was because part of me felt foolish, and the other part felt like *maybe* I should have given Parker more of the benefit of the doubt than I did. By not giving him a chance to explain, I hadn't shown him the respect I should've done, letting my stubbornness get the better of me. I'd been silly for so long, and now, he wanted me to rock up to his family's party and pretend as if the last five years hadn't happened?

Easier said than done.

'Please Atti,' he pleaded, jutting out his lower lip in a pout. 'If we're giving this thing between us another shot, then this is a part of the bargain. You know how close my family is. And I've got to show up there today, and I'd much rather show up with my favourite girl on my arm.'

'Oh, fine! You've twisted my arm,' I told him, shoving him in the shoulder a bit. 'Have we got to go to yours first so you can change?'

'Well, that. And I need to get Radley, too. He loves visiting his Nan and Grandad. He gets thoroughly spoilt there, you know what my mum's like.'

I nodded, instantly an image of Jane filling my mind, spoiling Radley with human food and extra treats. Jane had not one mean bone in her body, and when I thought about it, I had missed her and her motherly love for me. I just hoped she still felt the same towards me.

'Yeah, I can imagine she's a nightmare with him.'

'You bet! Now, before we go, come here and give me a morning treat.'

'A treat?' I laughed and placed a kiss on his cheek. 'What you got in mind, Mr Daniels?'

Parker gave me a cheeky grin and lifted the duvet to look at me.

'Let me show you...'

'ATTICUS, darling! Parker didn't tell us he was bringing you!' Jane exclaimed the moment the two of us and Radley made our way through the garden gate into the large green space.

'Hey Jane,' I said with a smile, shy and unsure of myself. I also felt self-conscious about my clothing—and my size. I was a bit bigger now than I was back in high school, and I worried that Parker's family would judge me. Especially his Auntie Carol, who had found herself sucked into a wellness MLM of late if her Facebook posts were to be believed. Pretty sure she'd be trying to sell me some weight loss shakes or supplements.

'Well, I can't believe my eyes! John! John!' she called across the garden to Parker's dad, who was manning the barbeque, tongs in hand. Jane wrapped her skinny hand around my elbow and pulled me alongside her, away from the safety of Parker's hand. I heard his small laugh as we went and put a reminder in my mind to get him back for this somehow later. Maybe I'd make him sit with my Uncle Darren at the next Allman family gathering. *Fudge biscuits! Now I was thinking further into the future with him.* Must remember that Parker is on a second chance, and therefore, not yet fully back into the fold. And by fold, I meant my family.

'It can't be!' John exclaimed, turning from the barbeque to face us both, tongs still in hand waving menacingly in front of his chest. 'Atticus love, is it really you?'

'Hi, John,' I replied, waving my free hand slightly. 'How have you been?'

'Oh, don't worry about me, love. Nothing much changes around here. Except you showing your face in our garden again, like the last however-many-years didn't happen.' He smiled wide, his jolly face causing me to reciprocate. John Daniels had always been friendly towards me, had always made me feel welcome whenever I'd come around here back in the day, and clearly he hadn't changed one bit. His dark brown hair had turned grey since I'd seen him last, but other than that, he was still *way* more attractive than any dad should be. People always told Parker they could see where he'd got his looks from, and those people weren't wrong. When the two of them stood side-by-side, it had quite the effect on people, especially the teachers and mothers at parents' evenings.

'So, Atticus, how come we're so lucky that you're here?' Jane asked, beaming just as wide as John while looking at my face with love and affection. They always were like second parents to me, and I'd missed them terribly.

Yet another relationship my stubborn arse had severed.

'Well...' I trailed off, looking around the garden to locate Parker and tell him with my eyes to get his butt over here pronto. I located him talking with his Auntie Carol, his face pillar-box red, and I could see she'd said something he didn't like. Most likely she'd mentioned to him that he could use one of her face masks or something. Sure that ego of his didn't like that one bit. I made the universal gesture for him to come over, and he made his excuses instantly and came to where I was standing with his parents.

I'd be lucky to ever get the smell of burning hot dogs out of this dress at the rate John was burning them.

'Darling,' Jane turned to him, craning her neck to look up into his eyes, 'I've just asked Atticus what she's doing here and she's being rather coy.'

'Mum. Dad. Atticus has finally listened to me, got her head out of that place where the sun don't shine, and has agreed to give me a second chance,' Parker said, with all the theatrics of a high school kid in their first school play as the lead.

'Do you mean it?' Jane asked, tears forming in her eyes as her brown bob bounces with each movement of her head. 'Really?'

'Yes, really,' I replied.

I was nearly knocked backwards when Jane and John both

leapt at me at the same time, both pulling me into a group hug, each of them using equal force and vigour.

'*Oof!*' My body let out a gust of air involuntarily.

'You two!' Jane said, removing herself for a second to pull Parker into this group hug with us. 'You don't even know how happy I am to hear it. A mother just knows these things and I've said to John many times that you two would work it out one day and give us grandchildren!'

I coughed as Parker sputtered, the two of us taken aback completely by Jane's words.

'What's going on over here then?' Cassie's voice reached my ears, and I felt saved. Cassie may be years younger than me, but we'd always shared a tight bond. *Must remember to ask her how her night out at Muse ended.*

'Hey!' I said to her, physically removing hands and arms from around me so I could jump out of the hug and stand beside Cass. 'Let's go catch up.'

I gave her that look. The one that said, *Save me.*

'Come over here, you can meet Zara's girlfriend.'

I nodded and gave Parker a quick peck on the cheek. He smiled and said, 'Go, have fun. I'll help Dad and try to save the sausages.'

'Think they're a lost cause, babe,' I said, and he nodded gravely. 'See you in a bit.'

'So, you and my brother are back on, ay?' Cassie wiggled her eyebrows, her long lashes fluttering with the motion. 'I'm happy for you.'

'You are?'

'Course. I've always wanted you two to end up together. To my eight-year-old self you two are endgame.'

I laughed at that. Sometimes it was easy to forget just how

young Cassie was when I first started coming around here and spending time with her.

'Well, that still remains to be seen,' I said.

'Trust me, girl,' she said with a serious look. 'That boy isn't going to let you go now that he has you back.'

We reached Zara and the person who I assumed was her girlfriend, and Zara's face lit up when she saw me. Instantly, it was as if an electric shock of warmth filled me, like my soul had forgotten a friend and had found them again. Zara had been a spinning instructor for the last couple of years, and whenever I bumped into her, I promised I would show up for a class.

Funnily enough, I never had stuck to that promise.

'Atticus! Girl, you are a sight for sore eyes.' We all laughed at her words as she pulled the girl at her side closer, pride radiating off of her. 'Atticus, this is my partner, Rula. Rula, this is Atticus.'

'I've heard so much about you,' Rula said, leaning in and placing an air kiss next to my cheek. Her brown almond-shaped eyes were filled with warmth and her wide smile split her face.

'You have?' I couldn't quite believe that. I'd always been friendly with Zara, sure, but not in the same way I had been with Cassie. 'All good, I hope?'

Honestly, what was it with us Brits using the same tired lines all the time? It was automatic, too. You couldn't help but make the joke that everybody expected you to make.

Everybody laughed at me, anyway, as if I hadn't just said something boring and cliché.

'Definitely all good,' Rula replied. 'Well, except for the whole avoiding Zara's spin class like the plague thing.'

I laughed good-naturedly, amused at being called out, but

also not too fussed by it. University took up most of my time, and then when I wasn't studying, the last thing I wanted to do was jump on a spin bike and have my leggings chafe on my thighs.

'Ha!' I said. 'I'm sure she's mentioned that more than once.'

For the next hour, the four of us conversed as if no time had passed at all. I was taken into the fold again like I'd never left it, and the fuzzy feeling it caused made me happy. I liked my family, but I'd never been close with them in the way I had been with the Daniels family.

It was like coming home.

Parker was my home.

Fourteen

Parker

'I RECKON the hot dogs are done now, Dad.'

I was being polite. *Done* was a bit of an understatement. The hot dogs on the grill were now burned to a crisp, the same colour as the charcoal underneath them.

'That's what gives them the smoky flavour,' Dad said, prodding my stomach with the tongs that I would have sworn were fused to his hand. He hadn't let them go since we'd arrived.

He was wearing a T-shirt with the words King of the BBQ in the centre and seriously, the man wasn't even wearing it ironically. He really believed that he had a skill with smoked meat.

He did not.

Everybody humoured him, though. It was easier.

'If you say so.'

Glancing around the garden, I spotted Atticus over with my sisters and Rula, looking as if she belonged there with them. Surrounded by Mum's petunias, she looked radiant.

The dress she'd chosen to wear today complimenting her perfectly. With other women, I never noticed things like what they were wearing—well, unless I focused on what they *weren't* wearing.

That thought led me astray, and I was no longer listening to whatever 'advice' my dad was spouting while I stood here silently.

Last night filtered through my mind. The places I got to kiss her, the moans she made, the overall feeling that I was with my soulmate overwhelmed me.

It had never been that way with anybody else. No matter how many women I'd slept with to get her out of my mind, none of them had ever measured up chemistry wise, or any wise for that matter, than my time with her.

'Atticus looks pretty today,' Dad said, and I nodded in response, not turning to look at him; my eyes transfixed on her as she laughed at something Cass said. They'd moved to sitting at a table and Radley was sitting by her feet, as she lazily stroked his head.

'She always looks pretty, Dad.'

'I'm proud of you, son. I always knew the two of you would work things out.'

'I didn't,' I said with a laugh. I'd hoped we would, of course I had, but I'd never really seen a way to make it my reality. Bumping into her at the wrap party had been fate. There was no other way to describe it. 'I never thought she'd listen to me.'

'You two are too stubborn for your own good.'

I looked at him, seeing the seriousness of his expression, and knowing that he meant it. And the thing was, I knew that he wasn't wrong. It was something we both needed to work on going forward if we were going to make this relationship work in the long run. And I wanted it to work out more than anything.

Turning back, my heart stopped beating for a second when I looked at Atticus again.

She was still sitting at the table, Radley at her feet, but now she had a baby in her arms. I had no clue who the baby belonged to, but what I knew was how seeing Atticus holding a baby made me feel.

It made me want the view I had to become a reality. A reality where Atticus was my wife, we had our own children, and Radley was our fur baby.

It was a vision of the future. My future.

And I would do everything in my power to make it happen.

'I HAD A REALLY good time with your family today, P. Thank you for making me come with you.'

Atticus and I were on the sofa together, her head resting on my lap as one of our favourite films played in the background. Ever since returning from my parents' house, everything had been so easy between us. The banter still flowed thick between us, but the biggest improvement was that the caring and affectionate side of Atti was back; a side that she didn't let many people see.

'I loved having you with us,' I whispered, trailing my fingers gently through her hair, loving the little sighs that were coming from her in response. 'It felt right, ya know?'

'It did,' she replied, nodding her head, causing a slight discomfort to come over me. We were having a nice moment. I couldn't ruin it because I had the self-control of a teenager. 'It made me realise how much I missed it. And how stubborn I've been.'

She moved her head, so that she was looking up at me, as I stared down at her intently, taking in every feature of her face. Every freckle.

'Yeah?'

'Yeah. If I'd just given you a chance to explain everything that happened with Alexa before, then I would have known you never cheated on me. And we'd probably still be together now, no issues whatsoever.'

'Sure,' I agreed. 'But you know what, Atti? What if that wasn't how it went? What if we'd stayed together, but then something else had torn us apart? Something that we couldn't come back from. I'm just happy I have you back now.'

'True.' She started to draw shapes on my arm with her fingertip, aimlessly drawing hearts and words. 'You're right.'

'Sorry, could you repeat that?' I teased. 'It's not often you say that.'

'Oh, shh!' she said, tapping my wrist. 'I'm just happy.'

But then she sat up sharply with a gasp, nearly knocking my nose with her head. Once sitting up, she turned to face me, pointing at me before she jabbed me in the chest with her finger.

'Hey! What was that for?' I asked, bringing my hand to my chest to cover the small area she just jabbed. 'You just said you were happy!'

'I am. But a thought hit me.'

'And what thought was that?'

'If you ever take your sweet-arse time to tell me something ever again, I'll make sure you regret it.'

I tried not to, knowing she wouldn't be overly impressed if I did, but I couldn't help but laugh at her face. The expression on her face was one of indignance, and her eyes had narrowed on mine.

'A, you wouldn't let me explain, remember?'

'Semantics, Daniels.'

I laughed, pulling her close to me, tucking her into my side. She burrowed in, placing her cheek on my chest, the two of us both inhaling and exhaling together. In sync.

'I know this is early days,' I started, wanting to get my feelings out into the open. 'But I've never been more sure of something, you know?'

Atticus moved, so she was facing me, blinking in silence, her eyelashes fluttering against her cheek, waiting for me to continue.

'I love you,' I said, reaching out to brush a strand of her hair from her face and place it behind her ear. 'Always have, and always will.'

The smile that took over her face was tentative, and unsure, but if I knew Atti the way I knew I did, then I knew she was feeling the same. It made sense that she was feeling apprehensive about returning the sentiment, especially with our past, but I knew she felt the same way.

She may not have realised it, but it was evident in the way she looked at me.

Heck, even back when she was pretending she hated me being in her space and my existence in general, the sparks still flew between us both.

'I love you, too,' she whispered back, blinking back tears. 'Just don't break my heart, okay?'

'I promise,' I whispered back.

I leaned in to place a kiss on her lips, slowly opening her mouth with my tongue, caressing hers in gentle strokes.

In the back of my mind, there was a nagging voice telling me I wasn't being completely honest with her.

But I swatted that voice away.

It was something to think about another day.

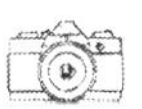

THE NEXT DAY, I was sitting on the sofa, Radley beside me, when Jackson walked through the front door.

'Honey, I'm homeeee,' he called out, making his way down the corridor into the open-plan living room. 'How's the weekend treating you?'

'It's Monday,' I deadpanned, raising a brow at him in question. I knew he'd been working a lot recently, but maybe he was overworked if he thought that it was still the weekend. 'Are you feeling okay?'

'I'm fine,' he replied, waving a hand to stop me from asking about him further. 'How was your time with Atticus?'

I grinned, the smile taking over my face without me even meaning it to. Just the thought of Atticus's big blue eyes, and dark brown curly hair, made me happier than I'd been in a long, long time.

'We're back together,' I told him, glee audible in my voice as I moved over slightly on the sofa to make room for him to sit next to me. 'Honestly, mate, we've had such a good weekend. I took her to the family party yesterday, actually. What were you doing? Mum said she'd invited you but you said you were busy.'

'Oh, I was helping Scar with her audition script. She's really improving.'

'That's good,' I said, sceptical about the amount of time they were spending together, but not wanting to say anything as I knew how closed-off Jackson could get sometimes. He would come to me when he wanted to talk. 'I've got a shoot on Wednesday, actually.'

'Oh, yeah? Who with?'

'Alexa,' I said with a grimace, and watched as Jackson's face mirrored mine. 'For that new brand that's been talking my manager's ear off.'

'Did you know you had a shoot coming up with her?'

'*Eurgh,*' I groaned. 'I remember Bruce saying something about it at my last shoot, but then I got distracted with an assistant.'

'Have you told Atticus about it?'

'About the assistant? Of course not,' I said, giving him an exasperated look. I was sure Atti had guessed that I'd been a playboy during this time apart, but I wasn't going to confirm it.

'Not about that, dickhead. No, I'm asking if you've told her about the photoshoot with *the* Alexa? The one she believed, for a long time, had ruined her life.'

'No,'—I took a big breath, certain he wasn't going to like the next thing I said—'I wasn't going to mention it to her.'

'Mate, do you really think that's a good idea?' Jackson's face told me all I needed to know. Yeah, it was a pretty bad idea, but I'd just got Atti back. I didn't want to give her a reason this soon into our new relationship to take a step back from me. 'If she finds out, she won't be quite so forgiving.'

'How would she find out?' I'd thought about it more than once and the photos wouldn't be published for at least six months, so by the time they were, Atti and I would be on better ground.

'Do you really want to start your relationship with a lie like this?'

'No, of course not. But it's not a lie. Just an omission.'

'If you say so,' Jackson said, 'but when it shoots you in the foot, don't blame me.'

I stayed silent, lost in thought about the dilemma I'd found myself in. Atticus was my endgame, and I didn't want to jeopardise it, simple as that.

After all, Atticus was my home.

Fifteen

Atticus

It frustrated me that since bumping back into Parker, and subsequently getting back together with him, I'd spent a lot less time focused on my studies and getting a job lined up for after I graduated.

I only had another two weeks left at university, or at least until my final dissertation had to be handed in, and I was floundering around like a fish out of water.

Somehow, I needed to find a way to stay afloat.

And to start that, I needed to scour the job websites and graduate forums to find positions I could apply for. It didn't have to be my *dream* job. Just *a* job. *Any* job.

Life piled up and time flew by so easily that I felt all out of sorts. Yeah, I was happy that Parker and I had reconnected, but I also didn't want to lose sight of my goals because of it.

'You gonna spend the day moping around?' Scar asked me as she entered the living room to find me draped on the sofa with a knit blanket covering me.

'No,' I groaned. 'I'll have you know I have a couple of big, important days ahead. Got some interviews at some places.'

I was being vague. And technically, I wasn't lying. I *did* have interviews lined up. Just not ones that were for jobs in my sector.

Not gonna lie, it was hard to find jobs as a history student that were both interesting and well-paid. Okay. Ones that I actually wanted to do, at least. I wanted to work in a historical house or palace, or something like that, sharing my love of history with the younger generations.

I supposed I could be a teacher, but I'd never really wanted to spend my time around teenagers trying to convince them that they should care about the past as it helps to write our future. It would infuriate me if they didn't take it seriously and I couldn't cope with that.

'What kind of interviews?' Scar asked, wrapping a beautiful grey cashmere scarf around her neck that had been a guilt gift from her mother for Christmas. She'd always had a strained relationship with her mum, and it was best not to ask about it ninety-nine percent of the time.

'Just some small tour guide positions,' I replied, brushing it off. I'd never been a fan of interviews.

One time, when I was still in high school, the school held an Interview Day where everybody was assigned an industry professional to do a mock interview with. I was assigned Mr Barclay, who was the dad of a boy in my class I couldn't stand. He'd always made fun of my name and my size and was just an overall grade-A dick. The moment I sat in the chair in front of him, my skin started to prickle with sweat and anxiety ran through my veins until it became all I could focus on. The entire interview had to be cut off early as I was ten minutes away from losing my stomach contents. So, yeah. Not really looking forward to tomorrow.

'You'll be fine!' Scar rubbed my leg in an affectionate gesture before putting her coat on. 'I'm off to work with Jackson today. He wants me to meet his team, see if they'll represent me.'

'That's exciting, Scar,' I said. 'Seems like Jackson is really helping you. Are you sure—?'

She cut me off and firmly said, 'No. There isn't.'

I nodded, accepting that she didn't want to talk about it. She would in time. I knew that much. It would get to a point where she couldn't contain it and would have to tell me before she exploded.

'If you say so.' I waved my hand in the air, dropping the conversation entirely. 'I might go visit Parker on his shoot later.'

I said it in a casual tone, trying to make it sound as if I didn't care. Hadn't fully committed to the plan, yet. But we both knew how false it was. I'd decided it before I said it.

The thing was, I wanted to see his job. Be around him in that space and watch him shine. He'd always been so good in front of the camera, the light always hitting him in the exact spot that made him look best, and—being frank here—I wanted to see that fine specimen in underwear more than anything. He'd told me it was an underwear photoshoot for a big well-established luxury brand, and I couldn't be prouder.

'Did he ask you to go?' she asked, and I sat myself up a bit, so I could look her in the eye now that she was making her way out of the apartment.

'No... Think I shouldn't go?'

'I'm not saying that,'—she shrugged—'just saying he might not appreciate it. You know how he gets when he's working.'

'Huh,' I said, sinking back down into the sofa cushion. 'Maybe you're right.'

'Drop him a text first? Just to make sure. You've not been back together long and you don't wanna rock the boat.'

'Yeah, you've got a point. Have fun today, tootsie roll!'

'I expect you to have all your fingers and toes crossed all day for me,' she said, giving me a short wave, before sweeping out of the room in a cloud of Chanel No. 5, her signature scent.

'You bet!' I called behind her before hearing the thud of the door closing behind her.

I looked around the room, taking in the framed photos of the two of us that cover the walls, and smiled. No matter what happened in my life, Scar was there for me. Always.

Scarlet always had my best interest in mind whenever she told me something, so I knew that she was probably right about me texting Parker before I arrived at the place he'd told me he'd be today.

It was still early. Maybe a nap first would put me on the path to making the right decision.

I'D awoken from my nap with a renewed sense of what I wanted.

And what I wanted was to go visit Parker and bring him some lunch. I knew that he loved the catering they provided for him, but sue me, I was feeling an overwhelming amount of love and all night I'd been reminiscing about our teenage years and it reignited that spark inside me. The one that wanted Parker Daniels. Not just sexually, and not just for now, but forever.

He'd always made my heart flutter in a way nobody else ever had. Even in the time we spent apart, I didn't have other relationships. I couldn't trust anybody after I thought he'd cheated on me with Alexa.

I'd not seen her since that night, luckily. Or at least, I'd not seen her in person.

She'd become a bit of a socialite since, or so Scar had told me. She'd spotted her a couple of times at industry parties and galas, always attempting to hang off the arm of the newest thing. Basically, the girl was desperate.

I'd been too scared to ask Parker if he had anything to do with her these days. It was a conversation we needed to have, but like other conversations we needed to have, I'd been putting it off. My inner voice had been calling me a coward for days, but it was as if I'd put a block on myself from voicing it all out loud.

I hated it, too.

Hey babe, are you hungry? Was thinking of stopping at Carlo's for some pizza. If you want, I can bring you some? I miss you.

I sent the text to Parker and wondered how long I should wait for a response before I just did it, anyway.

Throwing on some clothes, and getting out my apartment door, I bristled at the cold that seeped into my bones within seconds. Even though it was early spring, there was a chill in the air, meaning a coat and scarf were a definite necessity. My coat was oversized for two reasons. The first reason was so you could wear multiple layers underneath, and in the British winter, it became a godsend. The second was that it covered me more, like a large comfort blanket I could take outside with me.

The smell of Carlo's hit me before I turned the corner. Ever since they opened a few years ago, it had become mine and Scar's favourite place to go to get real authentic Italian pizza on the days that a large greasy one from the local kebab shop didn't sound appealing.

And on the days we didn't want to cook.

Well, and pretty much every day in between, too.

What could I say? We loved Carlo's.

The moment I opened the door, the bell over the door tinkled, alerting them to my presence. If I was an employee here, the bell over the door would irritate me to no end. The place was constantly jam packed with people, and the bell rang every thirty seconds or so—sometimes, it was a constant ringing sound that vibrated through you, leaving you feeling like the bell itself.

'Atti!' Gia called from behind the hostess podium, giving me a big smile.

'Hey!' I replied, making my way further into the restaurant and moving to stand out of the way of anybody entering to dine in. 'How's it going?'

'Good thanks! What are you doing here during the day?'

'I've come to grab a pizza for me and...' I trailed off, wondering how I should describe Parker. Was he my boyfriend?

It sounded so juvenile. We weren't teenagers anymore, and there wasn't much about Parker that felt like a *boy*friend. Or looked like one, either.

'...Parker.' I finished, as if that explained it. Gia's plucked eyebrows raised high on her forehead, disappearing behind her full fringe.

'*The* Parker?' she asked, and I nodded sheepishly. I'd forgotten that I'd opened up to her on a girls' night out one time. Let me just say, the wine was a-flowing, and so was my mouth.

'You've got a good memory.' I pointed at her, now feeling a bit awkward about it all. To cover it up, I pulled my phone out of my coat pocket and glanced at my lock-screen. It was a goofy selfie of the two of us and Radley, taken at Parker's place last weekend. We took it after we got back from his family's party, the two of us smiling wide and Radley's tongue lolling out of his mouth. I loved it.

'And you've got a lovesick expression,' Gia replied, tongue-in-cheek. 'I'm happy for you, girl.'

'Thanks!' I couldn't help the smile on my face. This last week, it had been a permanent feature on my face, not even leaving when I fell asleep.

'What pizza can I get ya?'

I thought about it, racking my brain for Parker's favourite pizza. He was pretty traditional when it came to his toppings.

'Pepperoni, please.'

'Pepperoni coming right up.'

ON ENTERING the warehouse where the shoot was taking place, I took a deep breath.

Parker had never replied to my text earlier, but I'd assumed it was because he wasn't allowed his phone while on set. He'd mentioned that I may not hear from him, as the shoot assistant would keep a hold of his phone and only answer calls in case it was an emergency.

What was the worst that could happen?

I got turned away, or Parker told me never to do it again in future?

Ultimately, I couldn't see Parker being angry at me. If anything, he was the one fighting me about how much time we were spending together. I believed we should spend every other night apart in order to have some space to reflect and make sure that this was what we both really wanted, but he'd been trying to convince me to nip it in the bud. He wanted to spend every free moment together, and although that was what my heart wanted, too, I was being wary. Not wanting to get my heart broken by him for a second time.

I didn't think my heart would be able to survive it.

'Excuse me, Miss?' A burly security guard asked me when I reached the main door to the area I wanted to be in. 'Can I help you?'

'Hey,' I said, trying to keep my voice from wavering with nerves. 'I'm here to see Parker Daniels. I'm his girlfriend.'

Huh. Clearly I didn't mind calling myself Parker's girlfriend. It was just the word boyfriend I had issue with.

'Name.' The man grabbed an iPad from the desk beside him, unlocking it and scrolling through a list of names. Oh, fudge biscuits. I hadn't thought to ask P to add me to his list.

'Er, it's Atticus Allman.'

I shuffled from foot to foot, holding the large pizza box out in front of me, the smell making my mouth water. I hoped it wouldn't be too cold by the time he got to eat it. I'd already eaten my margherita on the train here.

'Welcome, Miss Allman. Just through this door and to the left.' He gestured to the door to our right, and I nodded.

'Thank you.' I smiled and made my way through the door and followed around to the left like he'd told me to.

I could hear noises coming from across the way, a partition blocking my view from the voices and the camera shutters.

I'd never understood Parker's love for modelling, but I'd always been happy to support him in pursuing his passion.

Stepping around the partition, I made extra effort to be careful and step over the wires on the floor, not wanting to land flat on my face in front of Parker's co-workers. Couldn't have my clumsiness embarrassing me more than it already had.

What the...?

My eyes couldn't believe what they were seeing.

The pizza box landed on the floor, the sound reverberating through the cavernous space, having slipped from my hands involuntarily.

I blinked, adjusting to the lights. To the view in front of me.

My voice came out in barely a whisper at first, but I repeated myself enough times that eventually my one word carried across the space and made it to the ears of the person I loved most.

'Parker?'

Sixteen

Parker

'Oh, crap,' I whispered under my breath, Alexa still hanging onto me, her arms linked around my neck as we posed for the camera.

The look on Atticus's face made my heart drop down further than my stomach; it landed on the floor with a thump, and apparently, I was the only one who heard it.

It wasn't the only thing that dropped to the ground with a thump, either.

Atticus had been holding a pizza box, but it was now laying at her feet, forgotten.

'Parker?' Atticus asked, her bottom lip wobbling uncontrollably, the way it used to when she would cry out of anger or frustration. It wasn't often that Atti cried in front of people because she was sad, but I knew that was the emotion running through her at that moment. Sadness. Humiliation.

And I knew it was all my fault.

Jackson had told me to tell Atticus, and I'd been a stubborn arsehole, thinking I knew better. But deep down, I'd known all along it was the wrong decision.

Atticus had always given me her trust, both then and now, and I knew she was finding it hard to trust me again after last time. Yet I went and did this anyway, wanting to save myself from having a difficult conversation with her.

The real kicker?

I couldn't move. Couldn't acknowledge her.

The photoshoot was on a tight schedule and there was no way Bruce would allow me to halt proceedings because of my personal life. He'd call for lunch soon. Not like the man could go too long without eating. After all, he was known throughout the industry for being a great lover of food.

So I continued to pose, Alexa hanging on to me, and finished the shoot. I didn't look back over to where Atticus was standing, because I didn't want anything to distract me more than I was already distracted. It was a dick move, and I knew it, but it was as if my entire brain had frozen.

By the time Bruce called out that it was time for a lunch break, and I looked over to the spot where I'd last seen Atti, I knew she wasn't going to be there.

I'd known the exact moment she left. The air in the room changed, and a chill entered my body. It had even caused my skin to ripple with goosebumps, leading to them having to pause for a moment as they were showing up on camera and ruining the shot.

'Was that Atticus?' Alexa asked me, her tone one of disbelief once we'd made our way over to the catering table. 'Didn't the whole thing just give you *déjà vu*?'

She laughed, throwing her head back in what she believed was a seductive manner, but at that moment, it made my skin crawl. Alexa didn't know the gravity of the situation, as I hadn't mentioned anything to her before the shoot started. I'd barely spoke to her at all.

Over the years, we'd spent time together in a professional setting, but I tried my hardest to keep my distance otherwise, just in case I did ever get another shot with Atti.

'It was,' I replied tersely. I snapped at a passing assistant, 'Can I have my phone?'

The assistant gave me a brief nod and headed off at a fast clip, hopefully to locate my mobile. I needed to contact Atticus as soon as I could. I wasn't sure how long she'd been standing there staring at the two of us. To me, it lasted forever, but I hoped it was mere minutes.

'Somebody's feeling touchy today,' Alexa said with a titter. 'I didn't know that you were back with her.'

I ignored her, loading my plate high with carbs, knowing I would be on edge until my phone was in my hand and I could contact my girl. Talking to Alexa was the wrong thing to do. It would be like cheating, even though it was far from it.

'You not even gonna talk to me now, P?' She pouted, jutting out her enhanced bottom lip as she fluttered her eyelashes feverishly. 'She's clearly forgiven you, so what's the issue?'

'She *had* forgiven me,' I bit out through gritted teeth, no longer able to stay silent. 'But now she's probably creating scenarios in that imaginative head of hers.'

'Well, surely she knew I was here today. You must'a told her.'

I winced. God, if even Alexa thought that then I'd definitely done wrong, and hadn't treated Atticus with the respect she deserved.

'I...' I trailed off, and luckily, before I had to speak more, the assistant rushed back to me, brandishing my phone in triumph.

My hand darted out to take it from her, as I mumbled a quick, 'Thanks.'

There were multiple notifications, none of them important except one.

A text Atti had sent a few hours ago, about bringing me a pizza for lunch and that she missed me.

Oh, man. I'd messed this up big-time.

I pressed the call button and held my phone out, hoping she'd answer me but knowing she probably wouldn't.

There was a reason we'd only just reconnected.

Atticus was as stubborn as a person could come, and she'd never let me explain before, so why would she now?

And it irked me, really. Made me feel small, and like Atti didn't care about me as much as she should. She should be giving me a chance to explain. A chance to set things right without her stonewalling me.

The call disconnected, and I swore in frustration.

'She's not picking up, huh?' Alexa asked from beside me, her face amused and her tone mocking.

'Leave it,' I growled, moving away from the table, my plate of food forgotten.

I tried to call her three more times, but each time the call was disconnected after only a few rings, meaning Atti was blocking my calls.

'Models back on set!' A call went out through the warehouse and I rolled my eyes. There were only two models here today, yet they were acting as if it was fashion week. I took another glance down at my phone, hoping to see three dots in my chat with Atti, but there was nothing.

'Come on.' Alexa tugged at my arm, pulling me over to the next area we were needed in. 'She'll talk to you later.'

I nodded, but my stomach sank as I handed my phone back to the assistant.

I was in deep water.

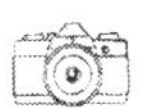

For the rest of the day, my mind was on everything but the modelling.

I couldn't stop thinking about Atticus, and how she must have felt walking in here and seeing what she did. I should've given her a heads up. Been a better boyfriend.

Told her the truth.

But I hadn't. And I couldn't turn back time to change things.

I had to accept what I'd done, and deal with the fallout.

'You ready to leave?' Alexa asked once we'd put our regular clothes back on and were wrapping up. I'd barely spoken to her for the rest of the day—luckily, modelling didn't require much talking—but now we were finished, she'd been talking to me non-stop.

'Yeah,' I said, hoping she'd hear the blunt tone and back off.

I had nothing more to say to her.

None of it was her fault, but even looking at her made anger flow through me. If she hadn't kissed my neck all those years ago, maybe things would be looking a little different today.

'Let's walk out together,' Alexa said. 'The assistant's have arranged a car home for us.'

I nodded, saving my energy for Atticus. I was going to get the car to drop me straight to her apartment without stopping at home first. I'd already texted Cassie to let her know I was going to be home a little later than I'd expected. She'd asked why, but I wasn't going to tell her any of it until it was sorted. Cassie had always loved Atticus, and I knew whose side she'd take. Plus, Cassie was too young when we split to know the true reason for it all. I'd hidden a lot from her, wanting to protect her, but also, I hadn't wanted to make myself look worse than I already did.

Alexa and I walked out of the warehouse together, her slightly ahead of me, while I kept my gaze down, my eyes transfixed on my phone screen.

I was still trying to contact Atti with no success.

The moment we stepped outside into the cold evening air, I knew something was wrong. Lights started flashing the second we left the door, and people were calling from all directions.

What?

'Parker! Parker!'

'How long have you two been together?'

'Alexa! How does it feel to be shooting with your boyfriend?'

'Parker. When did you know Alexa was the one?'

I shook my head, confusion fogging up my brain, as my eyes blinked every time the lights flashed in the darkness of the night sky. I loved the flash of a camera when I was modelling, but I wasn't in the mood right now for it.

From the smug expression covering Alexa's face, I could

tell that she'd been the one to alert the paps about where she would be. Or should I say, where *we* would be.

She'd set this up.

Wanting to gain herself some magazine miles at the expense of others.

'No comment,' I growled, pushing Alexa forward into the car that was idling at the kerb, waiting for the two of us. An assistant held the door open as Alexa got in first, then I slid in beside her.

Once the door closed behind us, I couldn't contain my anger.

'What the heck do you think you're playing at?' My blood was boiling and I could sense my cheeks were aflame. 'You knew Atti was already upset and now you've done this!'

'Oh, hush up. It was free publicity. It boosts us both and you know it.' She shrugged. 'Plus, she'll forgive you.'

'How can you be so sure?'

'She's forgiven you now,' she pointed out, and I had to stop the urge I had to say something really cutting.

'Yeah... Nearly six years later!' I instructed the driver to go straight to the girls' apartment, not caring that Alexa was now whining that she needed to get back for a very important phone call. 'Well, maybe you should have thought of that when you called the press.'

The two of us sat back in our seats, Alexa crossing her arms across her chest as I huffed impatiently, just wanting the car to move faster and get me to Atti's place.

The moment the car pulled up outside of her building, I leapt from the car, nearly hurting myself in the process, but carrying on regardless. I had to get to her.

Hours had passed now since she left the warehouse and I

wanted to see her. Hold her. Tell her how sorry I was for making her feel that way.

I rushed to their front door and knocked loudly multiple times, hoping that either Atticus or Scar would open the door.

When the door opened, it wasn't Atticus standing on the other side, but Scarlet. A very ticked off Scarlet, with an expression that would make lesser men quake.

'You've got some nerve showing up here,' she spat, prodding me in the chest with her pointer finger. 'How dare you, Parker.'

'Scar, you've got to believe me. It's all a big misunderstanding.'

'Oh,' she said, rubbing her chin, 'so Atticus *didn't* see you with Alexa draped all over you during an underwear photoshoot earlier today?'

'Well...'

'Save it.' She cut me off, then added in a low whisper. 'How could you? Why didn't you give Atti the heads up?'

'I thought I was doing the right thing,' I said, wanting Scar to understand but being fully ready for her to shut me down. We'd always had an on/off friendship, and if there was one thing Scar did well, it was protecting Atti and sticking up for her when she wasn't able to do it herself.

'You're an idiot, Parker Daniels.'

'Please, Scar. Please let me in. Or convince Atti to come to the door. I just need ten minutes of her time, max.'

She opened the door a fraction more, giving me a stern look as she did so.

'I mean it, Parker. If you upset her, or she kicks you out, then you leave pronto. I'm not messing around.'

'I promise,' I told her, meaning it. I wondered if Atti would even give me ten minutes, or if she'd ask me to leave straight away. There was only one way to find out.

I walked into the living room and saw Atticus sitting on the sofa. Her face was pale, her eyes red-rimmed and teary, and I knew she'd been crying for hours.

Steeling myself for her rejection, I took a deep breath.

'Atticus?'

Seventeen

Atticus

My heart was broken. It had been completely shattered by Parker Daniels once more, and this time, I wasn't sure if or when I would recover.

Walking into that warehouse today, and seeing him with Alexa attached to him like an extra limb, made all those memories rush back. It was the worst sense of *déjà vu* I'd ever experienced, and I never ever wanted to repeat it.

He'd lied to me. Concealed the truth, hoping I wouldn't find out until later. Or maybe he hoped I'd never find out at all. Either way, he'd deceived me.

'Atticus?' His voice called across the room as I looked at him standing in the doorway of our living room. I'd hoped Scar would kick him where the sun don't shine and that he'd leave without getting inside. Clearly, that hadn't happened.

'Parker,' I said, my voice dull, coming out in a croak. I'd cried all day and my throat was sore from the sobbing. Even I was sick of my own behaviour.

'Atti, you have to believe me, I—'

'You what?' I asked, not moving a muscle. 'You lied to me.'

'No, I never lied.'

'You didn't?' I asked, before turning on the television and showing him the images that were in front of us. Articles on Hive Mind about his and Alexa's relationship and how the two of them left the shoot together in the same car.

One of the headlines even read: Parker Daniels and Alexa Cummings' Secret Relationship! Six years and counting!

The first time I'd read that, a sickness had settled in my stomach. *Six years and counting?* Did that mean they'd been in a secret relationship ever since that night? Or maybe even *before* that night. I wasn't sure what to believe anymore, but one thing I knew was that I'd taken him back *way* too easily.

Parker's head turned in the direction of the screen, and his facial expression changed the moment he read the headline. His mouth opened and closed, like the spineless fish that he was before he managed to utter, 'Atti, it isn't what it looks like.'

'It isn't?' I asked, my anger rising with every syllable out of his mouth. 'Because what it looks like to me, Parker, is that you've lied to me. Once a cheater, always a cheater. Just this time, you've cheated *with* me. Are you happy now?'

'No,' he whispered. 'Atti, I'll never be happy without you, baby. Please, let me explain.'

'You've already had your chance, P. I already took you back once. I'm not ready to do this again so soon.'

'Please,' he said, his eyes filling with tears, the remorse emanating off him, but it was as if before they could reach me, they hit a wall situated directly in front of me. His theatrics, his falsehoods. They weren't reaching me where I was sitting. I couldn't let them, else my heart would shatter further.

'Leave.' My word was a demand rather than a question. I didn't want to stare at his face and doubt myself. Didn't want to fall into melancholy wondering whether or not I'd been too harsh to him. I would let him explain, but not yet.

This time, I'd let him. But it would be on *my* time. Not his. Not when he was the one who'd done the hurting.

'Atti—'

'Leave!' I raised my voice, the pain coming through, causing my voice to crack. The tears silently started to trail down my cheeks before I hastily wiped them away with the back of my hand.

Parker gulped, rubbing his hands on his thighs, looking like he wanted to say more but knew it was best not to.

But then he spoke anyway, ignoring his inner fight.

'Atticus.' He breathed in deep, his shoulders rising with the effort as he looked into my eyes intently. 'Last time, I let you go without trying hard enough. We were both too stubborn, and we wasted years being apart. But this time. This time, Atti, I'm not going down without a fight. We're going to talk about this and sort it out because we're endgame. You hear me?'

I sniffled, but stayed silent, not trusting myself to speak.

The resignation in his eyes cut me deeply; knowing I was the one causing him pain made everything worse, but I couldn't help it. My heart, and brain, had teamed up to ensure I wouldn't feel as much as I did last time.

After a minute of me staying silent, Parker shook his head and placed his hands in his pockets.

With one last sigh, he turned on the spot and slowly made his way out of the apartment, a dejected air following him as he did so.

The moment the front door closed behind him, I let out the biggest sob I'd been holding in.

After I left the warehouse, I'd taken a taxi straight back here as the pizza I'd devoured for lunch sat uncomfortably in my stomach, sloshing around with every turn of the vehicle.

The taxi driver was one of the worst I'd ever had, and on any other day, I would have probably given him a piece of my mind, but I was so sad I couldn't even tell him off with gusto.

'What did that arsehole say to you?' Scarlet asked, rushing into the room from her bedroom where she'd been hiding out while Parker attempted to speak to me. 'I'm sorry for letting him in, Atti. He just looked so sad.'

'I'm not mad,' I said with a sniffle. I looked once more at the TV, the headline and article still in place from where I'd been looking at them. I have my computer hooked up to the television, so when I got home I was browsing the internet, looking at things I'd never buy but would love to, to make me feel better. I was ready to think about maybe forgiving Parker, or letting him explain because I knew that I'd probably jumped to conclusions.

It would be stupid of me to let history repeat itself. I'd learned my lesson about not being so stubborn, and I was all ready to answer the last text he'd sent me, when a notification popped up telling me about Parker and Alexa.

I'd set up an alert for his name after the whole *waking up and seeing myself with my head in his crotch thing* happened. Before I did that, I barely had any reason to check out the Hive Mind website. It was a trashy tabloid that never told much truth, and I only even knew of its existence because of Scar. She would look at it to see what lies were being told in the industry—and the articles that weren't lies but were secrets revealed.

'Did you let him explain?' she asked tentatively, taking a seat next to me on the sofa. She reached out her arm so I could fall into her side, resting my head on her chest.

'Like you don't know already,' I said, making a small joke. I knew Scar would be standing outside the living room, listening in. I couldn't blame her either, because I would totally have done the same thing if our roles had been reversed.

'Fine,' she said with a short, deep laugh. 'How come you didn't let him explain?'

I pointed at the headline lazily, not moving my head to look at it again. If I did, I knew I'd cry even more. I hated crying where people could see me, but right now, with my head resting on Scar, I couldn't help myself.

'Oh,' she whispered, brushing my hair from my face and placing it behind my ear with a gentle touch. 'Right.'

'I just can't right now.' I sighed. 'I will eventually, but it's too raw. Scar, walking into that warehouse and seeing what I did. It just felt too raw. It was the past repeating itself and you know how I feel about that. My love of history stems from learning from the past, to ensure the faults of the past don't affect the future. Yet clearly I didn't take that to heart in my own life.'

No. Instead, I'd just let Parker Daniels walk all over me again.

'Well,' Scar said, taking my mind off my thoughts. 'Why don't you contact Alexa?'

'What?' I asked, sitting up fast, bumping my forehead on her chin as I did so. 'Ouch!'

'Message Alexa,' she repeated, as if it wasn't the most

ridiculous thing she'd ever suggested. She rolled her eyes at me and crossed her arms. 'Atti. I work in this industry, remember? Nine times out of ten, it isn't what it seems. Chances are, Alexa saw her opportunity for more publicity and she took it. Parker's more famous than her, after all. She's been a social climber for years, you know that.'

I nodded as I listened to Scar. As much as I hated to admit it, she had a valid point.

'Fine,' I said, begrudgingly. 'But how would I even contact her?'

'Just slide into her Instagram DMs,' Scar said, making it sound simple. Which, yeah, guess it was. 'Even if she has somebody handling her socials for her, I'm sure they'll tell her and she'll be intrigued hearing your name. Do you think she recognised you earlier?'

I ran my fingers through my hair in thought. I wasn't sure if she had remembered me, but I guess it wouldn't hurt to try?

'Okay,' I said with a big breath. 'Hand me my phone.'

Scar passed me my phone from where I'd left it upside down on our coffee table and I swiped away the notifications without looking at them. I didn't want to see anything that related to Alexa or Parker, and I sure didn't want to see any grovelling text messages from the man himself. Even if I was about to seek out Alexa's social media of my own volition.

I found her profile within moments and I smirked when I saw that she didn't have the blue verification tick. Not sure why, but I knew that would be annoying her.

Quickly, without hesitating too much, I tapped a quick message to her:

Hey Alexa, it's me, Atticus. Sorry to bother you, but I saw an article on Hive Mind about you and Parker, and I just wanted to reach out and get your side of it all? Thanks in advance.

I didn't have to wait long for the message to show up as seen, with the word typing appearing at the bottom relatively fast. Wasn't sure if I'd have to wait awhile or what, but then again, Alexa did strike me as the type of girl who had her phone attached to her like an extra limb at all times.

When a message reply bubble popped up, I was too scared to look at it. Scar nudged me in the side.

'You have to read it, Atti. That's the whole reason you reached out to her, remember?'

'Yeah, yeah.' I nodded. 'But I didn't actually think she'd reply!'

My breathing quickened, and sweat started to seep out of my pores in an unattractive way I had no control over.

'Well, she has,' Scar said, pointing out the obvious. 'So get to it, Finch.'

'Fine, fine.' I looked at her stern face and gave her a small smile. 'Anybody told you that you'd make a brilliant drill sergeant, Scar?'

'Somebody mentioned it once, but then I shouted at them to drop it and give me twenty.'

We both laughed, and like she had so many times before, Scar took away my worry and nerves just by being herself and taking my mind off it all by making me laugh.

'You ready to get over yourself and look now?'

I let out an exaggerated huff of annoyance, and muttered, 'Fine.'

My eyes focused on the words in front of them, but at first, they couldn't compute what they were reading:

Atticus, hey! Parker's my on/off boyfriend and has been for the last six years. You know how it is. One second, things are heating up, then the next they're freezing. We just got back together after some time apart and I'm so happy! Hope this clears everything up! Kisses.

After my third re-read, Scar took my phone from my grip and placed it on the oak coffee table in front of us gently.

'Are you okay?' she asked in a tentative manner. 'If it means anything, A, I think she's bullshitting.'

'You do?' I croaked, tears once again leaking from my eyes.

'I do.' She wiped a tear away from my eye and kissed my forehead. 'I've seen you two together these last couple of weeks, and I know how much he loves you. I may not be his biggest supporter after what went down, but we were teenagers. We're adults now, supposedly, which means both of you have grown from what happened in your past.'

I sniffled, still listening to her, as I drew patterns on my leg to distract my mind from going into a deep, dark pit of self-loathing and doubt.

'And Alexa is as mean spirited as they come. Always has been. She's one of those people who will do anything and everything in their power to come out on top—or at least to have all the attention. Don't let her get a rise out of you. Or make you upset.'

'It's hard.' My bottom lip wobbled as I tried to keep a hold of all of my emotions. 'Look at her and then look at me, Scar. She's a model, for fudge's sake. She's beautiful and I'm just a little dumpling that's always been lucky to have somebody like Parker interested in me.'

'Stop that, now!' Scar hit my arm in a soft slap that wasn't actually that soft. I narrowed my eyes at her, but she was unrepentant. 'Parker knows how lucky he is to have you. Why would he have been so bummed the last six years if you meant nothing to him, huh? You need to put on your confident boots and stop yourself from this spiral, Finch.'

'I'm not ready,' I whispered.

I wasn't sure if I ever would be.

It really was as simple as that.

Eighteen

Parker

'Another one!' I called out to the bartender over the loud chatter of voices coming from the others sitting at the bar. 'And keep 'em coming.'

The guy behind the bar rolled his eyes at me while he dried off the cocktail glass in his hands. I'd been a bit of a nuisance, and maybe I hadn't said please or thank you, but couldn't a guy catch a break?

I'd waited an hour for Atticus to message me after I left her apartment. Then another.

After four hours, I knew I couldn't stay home and wallow in self-pity any longer. I had to get out.

Cassie had promised to stay back with Radley until Jackson got home, and for once I didn't fight her on it or worry that Jackson would feel uncomfortable.

I didn't think about much of anything other than getting away and having a drink—or five—to help me to forget the look on Atti's face when I left her place earlier.

A large part of me understood her reservations.

Understood that the events of the past had warped her trust, and made her jump to conclusions, even if they were the wrong ones. And that was what pissed me off the most. Once again, she'd chosen not to give me a chance to explain. She just let me walk out of there without a second glance; no remorse whatsoever.

The bartender placed another whiskey in front of me, and I lifted it to my lips, savouring the taste on my lips before I gulped it down in one swig. I'd come to an exclusive bar in the city because I didn't want to have to deal with any fan girls right now.

A couple of weeks ago, I would have been thrilled that women threw themselves at me wherever I went. Would have welcomed it. But now even the idea of it made me feel sick. I didn't want anybody but Atti. Now I'd held her in my arms again, I couldn't imagine betraying her in that way by holding anyone else.

A commotion at the door caught my attention, and when I focused my gaze on the door, I could see Alexa Cummings and her entourage entering, all of them laughing and joking around. I had no doubt that whatever they were laughing about wasn't that funny. They just wanted the attention and would do anything they could to get it.

I turned away from the scene, not wanting to draw Alexa's attention. The moment I did, I would lose my temper and that wouldn't be good if any tabloid journalists were milling around. They were known to frequent these jaunts in the hopes they would spot something newsworthy.

'Another,' I said to the bartender when he caught my eye after he'd spotted my empty whiskey tumbler, but hadn't done anything to replace it. This bar had a policy that it wouldn't serve anybody too inebriated, but there was no way I'd had enough yet to be cut off. 'Actually, make it two.'

My skin prickled with awareness, my blood simmering to a boil, and I knew that Alexa had found me.

'Parker? Is that you?' Alexa whispered in my ear, pressing herself up against my back before leaning around to place a chaste kiss on my cheek. A growl left my throat in a low rumble, my annoyance towards her hitting an all-time peak. 'Darling, you didn't tell me you'd be here.'

'Knock it off,' I replied, brushing her hand away from my shoulder discreetly. I wanted her gone, but I couldn't cause a scene—there was too much riding on our upcoming campaigns.

'What's the matter? I didn't know the paps were outside, Parker, I promise.'

I scoffed, the whiskey stinging my throat as I listened to the lies coming out of her mouth.

'I find that very hard to believe.' I shook my head, trying to disperse the fog that was forming in my mind. Was this my fifth whiskey or my sixth? I couldn't remember—definitely not a good sign. It didn't stop me from picking up the full tumbler still in front of me and draining its contents in seconds, however.

'Why would I have done that, though? Especially as I knew Atti was mad at you.' Her voice was repentant, but her jade green eyes glinted with a darkness I couldn't decipher. I wasn't buying this vulnerable act. 'I hope it hasn't messed things up between you.'

'Oh, cut the crap, Alexa. You know it did. Wouldn't be sitting here otherwise, would I?'

With a nudge of her elbow, she made the guy in the bar stool next to me get up and move so she could sit beside me. Rolling my eyes, I glanced around the bar, taking in the sleek, modern lighting and dark wood-panelled walls. Anything to stop my eyes from being drawn to her.

Alexa may be an aspiring model, and she may be attractive in her way, but for me...she'd never interested me. Not once. No matter what Atticus may have thought for all those years.

'Why are you sitting here all alone at the bar? Thought you'd have grovelled enough that the two of you would be making up right about now.'

Alexa flagged down the bartender who, the moment he recognised her, came over with a smile on his face, showing all of his teeth. Clearly, he'd forgotten his annoyance towards me the moment he laid eyes on her. She had that effect on people. Her green eyes and daring, bright dyed-red hair beguiled everybody. Even Jackson wasn't entirely immune to her charms.

'I grovelled. She wouldn't listen,' I grumbled. 'Hive Mind posted those pictures of us and she didn't believe me.'

'Bummer.' She took a sip of her cocktail, pursing her lips around the straw, not seeming bummed by any of it. 'Atti never could see a good thing right in front of her face.'

I stayed silent, not giving her the reaction she was seeking. Alexa wanted to ruffle my feathers. Get me to act rashly in front of the cameras I knew she had poised all around the room.

'Want another drink?' she asked me, pointing at my empty tumbler. I nodded begrudgingly with my lips still firmly closed.

I needed to leave. I'd already spent too much time with her

today and I didn't want the press getting any ideas. Anything they posted would get back to Atticus, and that was the last thing I wanted.

The bartender placed my whiskey down in front of me with a small thud and I mumbled out a quiet thanks that I doubted he even heard over the din. The voices and noises were getting louder in the bar as the evening progressed; the place turning into more of a dancing club situation than an upper scale wine bar.

Just one more drink, then I'll be outta here.

My head pounded. My thoughts were scattered.

And when I attempted to open my eyes, they wouldn't cooperate. The bright sunshine in the room was too much for their delicate, thin skin.

Delicate thin skin?

What on earth was wrong with me this morning?

I didn't feel myself at all, and then I remembered the previous day, and it all flooded back to me. I'd intended to leave the bar not long after Alexa sat down beside me, but I couldn't remember if I actually did what I said I would. Anything past a certain point was a blur—a black hole of sorts—and nothing was coming to me.

Eventually, my eyes opened, and I breathed out a small sigh of relief when I saw that I was in my own bedroom at the apartment and not some strange place I didn't know. Small mercies and all that.

'Wake up, sunshine! Rise and shine!' Jackson hollered through the bedroom door.

I groaned, rolling over to face the door, wondering how long it would be until Jackson burst through the door, looking all bright eyed and bushy tailed. Closing my eyes again, I tried to get back to sleep, but within thirty seconds, the door opened wide and slammed against the wall.

Looking up, I found Jackson standing in the doorway, smiling wide, a cup of black coffee in one hand and a plate piled high with pancakes in the other.

'Somebody's cheerful this morning,' I said with a moan, eyeing him warily. Jackson only acted this way if there was bad news coming. 'Come on, mate. Lay it on me.'

I braced myself for the next sentence out of Jackson's mouth, hoping it wasn't as bad as I thought it would be.

'Last night was a heavy one?' he asked, walking towards my bed, his strides wide.

I sat up against the headboard and moved over so he could perch on the end by my feet after he handed me my coffee and placed the plate of pancakes on my lap.

'You could say that,' I replied tersely. 'But I don't remember much of it.'

'I guessed as much.' He clasped his hands together under his chin. 'Because you came home at 4 a.m. three sheets to the wind talking about how Atti will kill you.'

I sat bolt upright, moving so fast that my brain rattled around in my skull, making my already pounding head worse.

'And did I mention *why* Atti would kill me before I passed out here?'

I hoped I had. Of course I had. Jackson wouldn't have made me my favourite breakfast of chocolate chip pancakes if not. He saved them for special occasions.

'You did,' he said, his tone grave.

Not a good sign.

'And…?' I leaned forward and punched his shoulder. 'Don't leave me in suspense like this, dickhead.'

'You remember you bumped into Alexa, I assume?'

'More like she hit me with the weight of a freight truck, sure.' I shook my head, still annoyed at myself—and at Alexa. 'She took the seat next to me at the bar, and that's all I can really recall.'

'She must have set up the paparazzi again, because you were photographed leaving the bar together and getting into the same car.' He frowned, and I groaned, knowing that there was still more to come. 'In one photo, mate, she was tucked into your arm and kissing your hand.'

I groaned once more, feeling around blindly on my bedside table for my phone. No part of me wanted to bring up the gossip sites, but I knew I couldn't avoid it.

Atticus would be looking at these images, and I needed to know what I was going to be up against.

She'd said that we could talk soon.

Now I doubted she'd even allow that.

'It's bad, isn't it?' The question hung in the air, both of us knowing the answer, yet neither of us wanting to voice it out loud. Jackson may not have known Atticus for long, but he knew her enough to know this would hurt her. I felt certain that he and Scar had been in contact last night or during the course of the morning, talking about a way to knock sense into us both.

My phone screen was lit up like a beacon in my hand, the Hive Mind website pulled up, ready for me to look at.

I took a deep breath, calming myself down; praying it wouldn't be terrible.

Please. Please. My mind pleaded.

With one last steeled breath, I looked down at the front page that was glaring up at me. Instantly, my eyes were drawn to the gaudy neon headline flashing across the top of the page: Is Marriage on the Cards for Parker Daniels and Alexa Cummings? Click here for all the tea.

And somehow, it was so much worse than I expected.

'Oh, shit,' I said, not wanting to look further but clicking on the article, regardless. The picture showed Alexa hanging off my arm, smiling beatifically, looking the epitome of a woman in love. 'Assume you've seen this?'

'Yeah,' he admitted with a wince. 'I saw it.'

'I'm dead, aren't I?' I whined, putting my head in my hands. I could see my relationship with Atti slipping through my fingers before it ever had the chance to take off. 'She's never going to talk to me now.'

'She will,' Jackson said. 'She just needs time.'

'Has Scar told you that?' I asked before he'd even fully finished his sentence. He sounded as if he knew something I didn't. Some information that could be of major help to me.

'Scar may have mentioned it,' he said reluctantly. 'What are you gonna do?'

'I'm going to try and speak to Atti, of course. Call her. Message her. Send her gifts. Chocolates. Pizza. Anything and everything she loves.'

'Are you going to go to the apartment?'

'No,' I said, adamant. 'She won't let me in. I know Atti, and she needs time to see that maybe this isn't the way she thinks it is.'

'And how're you gonna convince her it isn't what she thinks it is?'

'I'm gonna set up an interview, clearing up that Alexa and I aren't a thing, for starters. Then I'm going to quit my job. Show that I'm serious.'

'Do you really think you should quit your job? P, you love being a model. It feeds your ego.'

I nodded, agreeing with his assessment of me. He wasn't wrong. I loved being a model. I loved the flashing lights of the cameras, and the adoration from my online following.

But I loved Atticus Allman more.

And I would do anything in my power to make her my girlfriend. My wife. My *life*.

It really was as simple as that.

Nineteen

Atticus

The moment I woke up the day after Parker left and looked at my phone, my heart sank even further. Further than I ever knew it could.

Pictures of him with Alexa were plastered over every social media outlet and tabloid site, causing a never-ending nausea to fill my stomach.

The next day, a parcel had arrived at my door (or so Scar said) with a handwritten note from Parker, asking me to give him the chance to explain everything. I ignored the note and opened the box to find an old Tudor coin that must have cost him thousands. It was beautiful, and it showed how much he knew me, but I couldn't bring myself to look at it for too long. I put it back in the box and went back to staring up at my ceiling.

It had been a week now since that day, and my stomach

still hadn't returned to normal. Each day, something new would arrive from Parker that I would ignore.

I hadn't even been able to eat properly, which, let me tell you, was a problem I'd never encountered before.

'Atti!' Scar called from the hallway, through my bedroom door, sounding pretty bored with my antics. 'Are you coming out today?'

I rolled over on my bed to stare up at the popcorn-covered ceiling, staying silent.

Over the past week, I'd barely left my room. I'd cancelled all the interviews I'd had set up, as I couldn't bring myself to get dressed that day, let alone sweat buckets in front of somebody judging me.

'Atti, please come out here,' Scar called again. 'We want to talk to you.'

My ears pricked like a dog's did when they heard an exciting word. She'd captured my attention, and she knew it.

'We?' I called back, moving to a sitting position, preparing to leave my room for the first time that day. 'Who's we?'

'Me and Jacks,' she replied, and if my ears weren't already at attention, they definitely were now.

'Jacks, ay?'

'Get your butt out here, Finch. I won't shout again.'

'Ay, ay captain!' I hollered back, a smile on my face—the first smile that had graced my lips in some time.

Scar and Jackson were sitting on the corner sofa together at one end, and I took my position on the other end while grabbing a fleece blanket to cover myself with for comfort.

Who knew what the two of them were about to say to me, and I needed something comforting to ground me.

'Atti,' Scar started. 'We need to talk.'

'You going to break up with me, too?' I quipped, poking my tongue out at her as she did the same back.

'Oh, ha, ha. Nice to see somebody still has their humour.'

'What do you want to talk about?' I asked, changing the subject, feigning ignorance, pretending I had no clue what they were going to say, though really, I could have said it all myself.

'Atti,' Scar started again, this time meaning business. Her eyebrows furrowed slightly as her eyes narrowed on me. 'You need to give Parker a chance to explain.'

'I—' I went to say more, but Scar cut me off with a sharp look.

'No.' She shook her head. 'I'm not listening to it anymore. I've let you have a week. Let you wallow and be sad and do all the things you do to make yourself feel worse, like watch *Atonement* and cry all night. But I'm done. You need to listen to us, and listen now.'

I swallowed, shocked to hear her talk to me in this manner. Scar and I had been friends since we were five, sure, but she'd never lost her temper with me. Not really.

My bottom lip wobbled as I fought my hardest to keep control of both my lip and my emotions. Everything felt so amplified. The hurt. The pain. All of it.

It had been a week from hell and I'd made myself my own worst enemy.

'It's hard,' I whispered, looking at both Scar and Jackson through my blurred vision. 'I don't know whether I can trust him again.'

'Why, though? He cleared up what happened in the past. And now you're not even giving him the chance to clear this up. He's sent you countless meals. Chocolates.

Historical memorabilia. All of it. And you've ignored everything.'

'I haven't been hungry,' I mumbled, feeling schooled. I'd wanted to enjoy the pizza from Carlo's and the burger from Carillo's—Parker knew my favourites and the way to my heart—but every time I went to take a bite, I was reminded that Alexa had draped herself all over him twice in one day. And after the message she'd sent me, and the headlines online, I couldn't decipher what was fake and what was real.

'Okay,' she said, placating me like a child. 'But that doesn't explain why you've ignored the sibling teddy bear he got for Henry. Or that you've not even looked once at the real Tudor gold sovereign. Atti, I know you. You want to hold that coin and imagine what it may have paid for in a former life. This isn't like you.'

'Scar, I'm scared,' I said, deciding to be honest; real and raw. 'What if he's lying to me? And he's been in contact with Alexa all this time.'

'He hasn't,' Jackson piped up, speaking for the first time since I'd joined them in the living room. His facial features were serious, his gaze assessing me. 'Atticus, I may not have known you long, but I've known Parker for a long time now, and honestly? It's pissing me off that you're not giving him the chance he deserves. All he's ever done is talk about you as *the one that got away*. Many times over the years, he's got drunk and talked about you. He loves you.'

A tear trickled down my face and I hastily brushed it away with my pointer finger. I'd thought I had no more tears left in me, but clearly my body had other ideas.

'Atticus, Scar told me what Alexa said to you,'—he gave Scarlet a stern look beside him before bringing his gaze back to me—'and it's total and utter bull. He's barely seen her and when he has, he hasn't interacted with her. She just saw her chance last week because they were shooting together and she knows his name is worth a lot more than hers is in the press's eyes. She saw her opportunity, and she stole it.'

The thing I didn't say to Jackson was the fact I'd come to this conclusion myself three days or so ago. It was hard to accept that you were wrong—that you made an arse of yourself by going on assumptions instead of facts—and to then make amends.

'He's trying his best, yet you've been ignoring every call. Every message. Email. Direct message.' Jackson looked resigned, and my heart twinged. Jackson would only know all of this because Parker had told him. Or Scarlet had. Probably both.

'Today's the last day you're getting away with that, missy.' Scar nodded, pointing at me. 'I'm not letting you do it to yourself any longer. You deserve to be happy. And Parker Daniels makes you happy.'

'What if he doesn't, Scar? What if he takes my heart and breaks it in two and then gives it back? Or worse. He takes my heart and doesn't hand it back.'

'If he takes your heart, and doesn't hand it back, Atti, then that means he'll hold it and cherish it and be yours forever more. Why wouldn't you want that? I know sixteen-year-old Atti would be kicking you in the bum right now.'

I laughed at her choice of words, knowing she spoke the truth.

'It's all a lot easier said than done, isn't it? I just feel so stupid. Mostly for letting Alexa take me for a ride like that.'

'You've been stung before, so I get it,' Scar said. 'But now you need to trust *him*. You're grown now. The two of you need to talk.'

I knew Scar was right, and as I watched Jackson nod his head in agreement, I knew even more that I'd been a stubborn fool.

Picking up my phone, I sent a message to Parker, hoping he'd read it and reply. Not once this week had he stopped trying to get a hold of me, so I hoped he still wanted to hear from me.

P. I'm sorry. Are you free to come over tomorrow night? I'd like to talk.

If he came over the next night, I'd have time to shower and wash my hair—something I'd failed to do this past week—and prepare myself to be in his presence again.

Yeah. Twenty-four hours would do me nicely.

'What are you doing here?' I blurted out, opening the front door to find a tired looking Parker.

I'd only sent my text message an hour ago and hadn't heard back from him yet. Clearly, he'd seen it and come straight over.

His hair was ruffled, like he'd been running his fingers through it since I saw him last, and his eyes had prominent dark circles underneath them like he hadn't slept a wink in days.

'Atti, please can we talk?' he pleaded, looking me in the eye. 'I just need five minutes. Baby, let me in.'

His blue eyes seared me, down to my soul, and all I could do was give him the tiniest nod of my head in response, opening the door wider for him to slip past me. I made sure to move back so that his body wouldn't touch mine, but even just feeling the heat from his body made a chill travel through mine. It may have only been a week since I saw him last, but time had elongated while I lay on the sofa feeling sorry for myself.

'Would you like a drink?' I asked, following him down the hallway, taking him in from head to toe from behind. Through the tight white T-shirt he was wearing, you could see every muscle of his, each one defined and singing to me to lick each ridge with my tongue.

Down, girl. Let him grovel first.

'No, I'm fine, thanks,' he mumbled, looking over his shoulder at me briefly before continuing onwards. The fact that he wasn't pandering to me, and trying to kiss my arse, made me pause. I'd got so used to Parker wanting to make me happy that I didn't know how to act around this Parker.

Silently, we made our way into the living room. Parker sat down on one end of the corner sofa and me on the other. The frigid temperature in the room wasn't solely because of the time of year and I shivered, hugging my arms around myself to try and keep the warmth in.

'So...' I started, hoping he'd pick up the conversation soon. He'd shown up here wanting to talk to me, so I'd assumed he would start talking the moment he had an opportunity. But instead, he was leaning forward, resting his elbows on his knees, looking at me with a pensive expression on his face. 'You wanted to talk to me?'

'I've been trying to talk to you for a week,' he said before swallowing. His Adam's apple bobbed with the movement and I found I couldn't look away. Anything to distract me from the pain in his eyes and the hurt I'd caused him. 'But you wouldn't return my calls.'

'I wasn't ready,' I replied. His accusation hit me where it cut the deepest. 'I needed time.'

'And is this a convenient time?' His tone was slightly mocking, and I shrunk in place; like a wilting flower that had been picked by some obnoxious kid and left to die.

'I guess,' I squeaked out, feeling uncharacteristically shy in front of him. 'You're here now.'

'I can leave.' He made moves to stand up, rubbing his hands on his thighs before placing his feet further apart on the floor.

'No!' I shouted, feeling my bum lift off the sofa as I made the move to stop him with my body if I needed to. The smug smile that overtook Parker's face caused a flush in my cheeks.

Dick had played me.

'Nicely played, Daniels,' I said as he laughed. The sound was like music to my ears, as I hadn't heard it in so long. How had I let him leave my life for the seven whole years? How had I been so stubborn that I couldn't get over myself and have him and his infectious laugh around me at all times?

'Sometimes, A, you need a kick.'

He wasn't wrong. That was how he'd convinced me to date him back in the day. For a year he'd asked me out, tried his hardest to woo me and win me over, yet I thought he was joking. So after a year, he'd asked another girl out. Scar, to be exact. And of course, now I knew that she'd been in on it, but at the time, I'd been livid. I was even more livid when she'd said yes.

But did it spur me on into accepting my attraction to him and accepting his date request?

Yes, yes it did.

'True,' I said, twiddling my thumbs. 'Where's Radley?'

'With Cass,' he replied, and I nodded. Rubbing my arm to distract myself, I looked around the room before focusing on the framed pictures in the hallway of me and Scar.

The tension came back as we each waited for the other to speak, neither one of us knowing how to start the hard conversation to come.

'Atti,' he blurted out at the same time I said, 'Parker.'

'You go first,' he said, gesturing at me.

'Okay,' I replied, and took a deep breath, inhaling air in through my nose and holding it there for a second or two before exhaling out of my mouth. 'I'm sorry for not letting you talk last week. I shouldn't've shut down on you the way I did.'

'You're right,' he said. 'You shouldn't have.'

His smile was cheeky, and the way he was getting a kick out of me eating humble pie caused a smile to form on my face, too. He sat back, crossing his leg over his knee, the picture of nonchalance. The casual air surrounding him did help with my anxiety, though. In a way he'd perfected, he was putting me at ease.

'Right,' I agreed. 'I also wanted to open up about why I've ignored you this week.'

He nodded, waiting for me to continue.

'So. Don't kill me.' I looked into his eyes, the nerves creeping back in now that I had to tell him I believed some wannabe model who'd never liked me over him. 'But I messaged Alexa after you left on Wednesday, and she replied.'

Parker tensed up, leaning forward with one of his eyebrows raised, the disbelief evident in every movement.

'Sorry,' he said, running his fingers through his rugged hair, 'but did you just say you messaged Alexa? After I left here?'

'Yeah,' I confirmed. 'And then the next morning when I woke up and saw even more pictures of the two of you, I sort of convinced myself that she'd been telling the truth. That you were some big liar who was keeping me on the side while you were on a break with Alexa.'

'And you seriously think that low of me?' he whispered, the hurt hitting me like a million pieces of tiny shards of glass had been catapulted in my direction. Hearing him sound so small, so disappointed in me, was horrible.

'No,' I whispered back, shuffling over on the sofa so I was a little closer to him. Not wanting a gap between us, but knowing that we weren't yet in the place for me to boldly seat myself next to him. I hadn't earned that privilege. 'I was a dick.'

'You can say that again,' he said with a derisive laugh. But then he caught himself. 'I'm sorry, I shouldn't laugh because I've clearly done something wrong.'

'No!' I shouted, this time standing and taking the seat next to him so I could place my hand on his thigh. That touch. It was everything.

The spark of electricity that zapped between us brought life back into me.

I'd been a zombie for the last seven days, and now—even though I still looked like a zombie—I was feeling alive once more. Like the best me I could be.

And it was all thanks to Parker.

'P, aside from not telling me about your shoot with Alexa,

you've done nothing wrong. It's all me.' I hated how weak I sounded, but really, there was no weakness in honesty. Not when you were being honest with the person you loved more than anything else.

'The fact you even believed her for a millisecond, let alone multiple days, cuts me deep. And it tells me that I haven't made it clear to you how much I love you. Because I do. I love you so much that it pains me when I'm not around you.'

Tears sprang to my eyes at his declaration. My heart stuttered, skipping a beat with each word he uttered. He placed his hand on top of mine and squeezed.

'A, you're my world. You always have been, even when you didn't want to know.' He tucked my hair behind my ear before he wiped a tear before it completed its path down my cheek. 'I hate that you feel so insecure about my love for you. My devotion to you. Seeing you bring yourself down, it sucks.'

I nodded, sniffling loudly, but trying not to let the tears overtake me.

'I love you,' I whispered. 'Forever and always.'

Twenty
Parker

'I love you,' she whispered. 'Forever and always.'

It was all I'd wanted to hear when I set out for the apartment the moment I got Atticus's text. Well. That, and an apology.

I wasn't going to wait until tomorrow to have this cleared up. Not if it meant I could have one extra night with her in my bed, laying in my arms, close to my heart.

'I love you, too.' I leaned forward and placed a kiss on her cheek, and then on her temple. I poured all of my love for her into the action, not wanting to stop the conversation, but wanting Atticus to realise that I wasn't lying, or fobbing her off. Or anything else she may have thought since Alexa whispered those lies into her ears.

Trust Alexa to mess up the best thing to happen to me, and then see me in a bar and make the situation worse. She knew when she found me at that bar that Atti thought the worst—she'd already messaged her to 'confirm' our relationship status.

'But you have to promise me one thing,' I said, hardening my tone a little, to let her know I meant business. I was serious, and I wanted her to hear me. Not just hear me. But take it in, absorb it, and accept it.

'What?' she asked, her tone breathy with an underlying hint of nervousness.

'You have to promise me—and I really mean it this time—you have to promise me that you will talk to *me* and nobody else before you pass your judgement. Because this is the last chance I'll give you, Atti. It hurts me that you'd think so low of me,'—she opened her mouth to speak but I continued, making sure she didn't say anything—'and I don't think I can deal with that sense of betrayal a third time.'

'It makes me feel so crappy, knowing I made you feel like that,' Atti said, the tears still slowly leaking from her eyes, making my gut clench.

'I don't want you to feel crappy.'

'I can't help it,' she cried. 'I've been such a stubborn arse.'

Laughter barked out of my mouth involuntarily, and I told her, 'You can say that again!'

She joined in the laughter, throwing her head back, drawing my eyes to her features that I loved so much. Everything about her was perfect for me and it killed me to know she sometimes thought of herself as 'dumpy' or unattractive. If I could do anything, I'd take those insecurities away from her. Toss them in the ocean and let them drown.

I hoped that by loving her right, eventually she'd see herself the way I saw her.

'But you forgive me?' she asked, her wide blue eyes staring up at me through her teary lashes. 'Because I really am very sorry.'

'I know you are.' My head pressed onto hers, holding our connection, our eyes locked on one another. 'And you can stop beating yourself up now. I forgive you. This week I've been walking around without a heart, because I left it with you.'

'You make my heart flutter. You know that, don't you? That's why you say these kinds of things to me.' She pushed my shoulder, but there was no force behind it. Her smile was small; shy and timid, yet so beautiful. 'You're a charmer, Parker Daniels.'

'I am, am I?' Tilting my head, I placed my lips on hers, catching her off guard. A slight gasp left her mouth, the noise heading straight to my dick, who hadn't been awake since the last night he spent with Atti before everything went wrong. 'Well, how about I charm you some more?'

Her hand started to wander, moving from my thigh, until it landed on the place I wanted it most. She rubbed my erection on top of my jeans and the friction caused him to twitch.

I gripped her hand in mine, not wanting her to feel what I had hidden in my pocket, and put it in my mouth to give it a little nip.

'I'm taking you to bed,' I told her, standing up and pulling her up alongside me. Once she was standing, I lifted her into my arms to carry her to her bedroom.

'Put me down,' she screeched, attempting to hit me so I'd let her go, but I had no intention of doing so. 'P, I must be so heavy!'

'Stop smack talking yourself, A. I won't tell you again.' I pinched her bare thigh as her robe rode up to reveal her pale skin. I hated the way she put herself down, and even if it was the last thing I did, I would spend my whole life helping Atti change the way she saw herself. I wanted her to see herself how I saw her. Which was beautiful, funny, witty, charming, and so many other adjectives I couldn't even list them all. Seeing her do this was horrible and I would end it.

Once we were in her bedroom, I placed her gently down onto the edge of the bed, so that her legs were hanging over the edge and touching the floor. Atti looked stunning, her robe barely closed, with her brunette hair in a high ponytail that drew your eyes to focus solely on her face. Her blue eyes were looking at me with wonder, and if I knew Atti, she was curious about what I would do next.

I pulled my T-shirt over my head, then pulled down my jeans and my boxers, my hardened dick standing straight to attention.

'Come here,' she whispered, licking her bottom lip, and I knew I would like what was coming next. I walked towards her in large strides, until I stood in front of her, her head at the perfect level.

Tentatively, she leaned forward and licked up my shaft, making it harder than before. Her hand grabbed my dick so she could put my entire length inside her mouth, her lips firm as she bobbed up and down.

'God, Atti,' I groaned, the pleasure of her touch overtaking me. In the past, when other women had done this act on me, it was Atti's face I'd envisioned when I looked down. That may make me sound like a prick, but it was the truth. Every time I'd had sex with somebody else, all I had done was compare them to Atticus.

And now she was back in my life—for definite this time—I couldn't believe my luck. That I was looking down on her gorgeous features, her magnetic blue eyes staring up at me, giving me that connection we both craved.

I gripped her ponytail, curling it around my palm, and with only a little force, pushed her forward a little further. Within moments, I slowly pulled her off, her mouth making a popping noise as she released my dick from her mouth's suction.

'I want to come inside you,' I told her, bending down to place a kiss on her lips. The kiss was slightly salty, and I loved tasting myself on her lips; claiming her as mine.

My heart soared at that thought. *Mine. Atticus Allman was all mine, and I was never letting her go.*

Atti laid down, parting her legs seductively, wanting me inside her. I moved onto the bed, placing myself beside her, swirling patterns on her stomach, before trailing my hand down to the apex of her thighs. Slowly, I pushed a finger inside of her, feeling her arousal coat my finger in an instant. I pushed a second finger inside, thrilled when her back arched, letting me know how much she was loving my touch.

As much as I pretended I was calm and collected, when it came to Atti, I was anything but. I wanted to make her feel good. Wanted to erase the years apart from her mind until all she could think about was me; us. And our future together.

Atti started to moan, her body writhing from my touch, as her orgasm reached its peak, sending her over the edge. Her moans were one of my favourite sounds beside her laughter.

After she came down, I removed my fingers and moved myself to rest above her, the head of my cock about to breach her entrance.

'You okay?' I asked, watching her eyes for any sign of a lie.

She nodded, her cheeks flushed, a beautiful shade of pink covering her breasts.

'I'm better than okay,' she whispered, a shy smile overtaking her face.

With one thrust, I sank inside her, loving the way she felt clenched around my dick. Every time inside her felt like the first time. Everything about her turned me on and set my body on fire. I loved her more than anything in this life, and I knew that this was the start of our forever.

I thrusted hard and fast, wanting to get us both there, wanting us both to lose control together. When I felt my balls tighten, I pressed on her clit with my thumb, hoping to push her over the edge with me.

'Yes,' I hissed out, as I lost control, exploding at the same time she let out a, 'God!'

Her mouth opened wide as she rode out her orgasm. I watched her in awe, feeling like the luckiest man alive to have her fall apart because of something I'd done.

'I love you,' she whispered the second she'd caught her breath back. I leaned down to place a firm kiss on her mouth, all my love for her leaving me in that kiss.

'I love you, A. So damn much. And I will spend my life showing you that.'

The two of us woke the next morning, side-by-side in bed, all possible limbs touching.

During the night, Atti had laid her leg over mine, pulling me closer to her, and I loved every second of it. Even if it made me sweat the entire time and feel a tad claustrophobic.

'Morning,' she whispered, kissing my pec.

'Morning,' I parroted back, placing a kiss on her head,

inhaling her sweet scent as I did so. There was something about smelling people's heads, wasn't there? Something that brought comfort you could take solace in.

'How are you feeling?'

'On top of the world,' I said, kissing her head multiple times, before laying back to stare up at her ceiling. 'Do you ever try to find patterns in the ceiling?'

'All the time,' she replied with a laugh. 'Swear I saw an elephant up there the other day, but I haven't been able to find it since. The second you look away, it changes when you come back to it.'

'Right!' I agreed, happy to be feeling so carefree with her at my side. Playful Atti was always a good sign—especially in the mornings. Usually, she couldn't function before her first cup of coffee. We used to joke that she was the beast, and I was the beauty before her dose of caffeine. 'Pretty sure I just saw a panda.'

'You did not,' she said, prodding me in the stomach as she did so. 'You're so full of it.'

'Made you smile though, didn't I?' I squeezed her towards me, loving the feel of her skin on mine. Now that I'd gauged her mood, it felt like the perfect time to bring up my future as a model. 'A?'

'Yeah?'

'How would you feel if I quit?'

'Quit what?' She propped herself up on her elbow so she could look me directly in the eyes. 'What are you chatting about?'

'Quitting.' Then I clarified. 'Modelling.'

'You want to quit?' she asked, narrowing her eyes on me, scrutinising my face for any sign of a lie. For her, my statement had come from out of the blue, but ever since Alexa pulled her stunt last week, it was something I'd been mulling over.

I didn't want Atticus to feel insecure, or worried, about the shoots I took part in. The other models I spent time with. The past six years, it hadn't bothered me. Heck, I'd enjoyed meeting all the women. Spending a night with them, then never seeing them again.

But that wasn't my life now.

Atticus was.

'Don't be so silly, P.' She flicked my nipple, narrowing her eyes until they were tiny slits on her face. 'You love modelling.'

'I know,' I said with a nod of my head. 'But I love you more.'

'I get that, and I love that you'd be willing to quit for me. But I don't want you to.'

'You don't?'

'No, because I know it makes you happy. And yeah, I was a bit blindsided finding you with Alexa in that way, but if you'd *talked* to me beforehand, it wouldn't have been as much of an issue.'

'So, you're telling me if I *had* told you about Alexa, you'd have been chill?' I found that a little hard to comprehend. Chill wasn't a word I'd pick to describe Atticus.

'Oh, heck no. Not quite,' she said with a laugh, then stressed, '*but* I would have got over myself. And I still would have brought lunch, and said hi.'

'I'm sorry I didn't trust us enough to talk to you about it.'

'It's okay. Just don't ever do it again,' she said, simply, as if that was all there was to it. 'And I'm not gonna lie. I may be a little sour if you work with Alexa, more because of how she's acted this week, not because of what happened all those years ago. But I'd never make you feel bad about it.'

'How about we compromise, then? I won't work with her unless I can't get out of it, yeah?'

'Sounds good to me!' Atti laid back down, once again resting her head on my chest, as she drew patterns lazily on my abs.

'I have something for you,' I said after we'd been laying in silence for at least ten minutes. Before I left my apartment yesterday, I made sure to grab something I'd been holding on to ever since we were seventeen, and was just waiting for the right time to give it to her.

'You do, do you?' she asked, waggling her eyebrows at me.

'Not like that,' I said, appreciating her dirty mind but not wanting to get side-tracked by it, 'but maybe later if you ask nicely.'

'Then what is it?' She sat up, holding the duvet under the arms to cover herself, looking at me expectantly. With a laugh, I sat up too and reached down for my discarded jeans from where they'd fallen on the bedroom floor. Rooting around in the pocket, I found the box I'd been looking for.

'So, remember back when we were young and dumb?' I asked her, holding the box behind me out of her view. 'And we were adamant that we were endgame? Even when your parents were a little sceptical, we wouldn't listen. Thought we knew better.'

She nodded, waiting for me to continue.

'Well, back then, I got something for you. I used all the savings I had for this—well, every penny I had that we didn't spend on bowling, at least.'

'Call me intrigued...' she said, making grabby hands

towards mine, her impatience at the unknown rearing its head. 'You gonna show me?'

'I am, but just remember. Young Parker didn't have anywhere near as much money as older Parker does.'

'P,'—she looked me in the eye—'I've never cared about whether you had money or not.'

'Of course, I'm just laying the foundation.'

'Okayyy?' Her eyes were alight with excitement, and although I knew it was killing her not knowing, I wanted to tease her a little. Drag it out just a little longer.

'Close your eyes,' I demanded and in an instant, she did as I asked, not even questioning it once. *Eager beaver.*

'Atti,' I started, my tone low. 'The day I got this, I knew you were my forever. All I wanted was to finish university, and come back to you so we could build a home together. Roughly a week before I left for uni, I went to the local jewellers and got you this.'

I placed the box in her open palm, having opened the lid while it was behind my back, and took a deep breath.

'You can open your eyes now,' I told her. As eager as expected, Atticus's eyes opened and blinked a couple of times, her eyes adjusting to the ring box in her hand. She gasped and opened her mouth, but before she could start talking, I spoke again. 'This isn't me asking, just so you know. This is my promise to you, that one day I *will* ask. I *will* make you my wife, Atticus Allman. And we will have that life we always envisioned. A home, with our dog Radley, and our son Henry and then whatever other children we may be blessed with. So, what do you say? Will you promise me forever?'

Tears filled her eyes, but this time at least, I knew they were happy ones. Her bottom lip wobbled, and my heart twinged at the sight of it. As much as I didn't like to see her cry, I had to admit, she looked mighty cute when she did.

'Of course, I promise you forever. It's all I've ever wanted.'

She took the ring out, letting the box drop down to the bed, before shoving it on her ring finger on her left hand.

'You know, teenage Parker did good.' She admired the ring, moving her hand around in all different directions, making the diamond in the centre catch the light and sparkle. 'I love it.'

'And it will look so much better when it's joined by your real one.'

'Have I mentioned that I love you, P?'

'I love you, too,' I whispered. 'Forever and always.'

Epilogue
Parker

Three months later:

I'd been nervous all day.

Atti had absolutely no clue what lay in store for her, and that just made everything even more nerve-wracking.

All of our friends and family were aware that today was the day I would ask Atticus to be my wife, and were in on the plans for the day. No doubt that would annoy her, seeing as Atti always hated being the last to know something, but I also knew she loved a surprise and pretending she didn't.

For as long as I'd known her, Hampton Court Palace was one of her favourite places to visit. Atti loved the history, the gardens, the experience...all of it. It made total sense to me that she'd gone for a degree in history and now that she'd finished; she was hoping a job would open up here soon.

I knew the moment I'd suggested we come here for a day

trip she'd been a tiny bit suspicious. Especially as today was the anniversary of the day we first started a relationship way back when.

It wasn't that I didn't support her love of history, I definitely did, but it wasn't often I actively opted to join her on a palace escapade. For me, a trip to a theme park was more my speed. At least there you got a shot of adrenaline. When I'd mentioned it to her though, all she said was, 'History *is* an adrenaline thrill to me, P. Standing in the same spot as so many important figures of the past sends a thrill through my bones. Makes me feel alive.'

I just nodded, the smile on her face making one cover mine. Seeing her happy was one of the best things and, hopefully, that smile would get wider as the day went on.

'Where to next?' I asked her, hoping that she wouldn't want to wander the halls for much longer, as our family and friends were expecting us out in the gardens in an hour's time.

'The chapel,' she said, without even having to think about it. 'It's beautiful there.'

'Can't say I remember,' I told her honestly. After all, it had been some time since I'd traipsed around here in her wake. When I visited to scope out a perfect spot with Scar and Jackson a couple of weeks ago, we only visited the gardens.

At a quick pace, the two of us made our way to the chapel, with Atticus leading the way like a tour guide. All she was missing was the giant umbrella they always carried to show where they were.

On entering the chapel, Atticus's eyes widened and a beautiful, happy smile covered her face until she resembled the Cheshire Cat. The awe on her face moved me. It always did when I saw her passion. Her love of the past. Of the people and the events that would have taken place in this very room.

'Can't you feel it, P? The atmosphere here?' She surveyed the room, taking every nook and crevice in, even though she'd seen it all before. Pretty sure she even owned multiple books with images and information in, too. 'This ceiling is stunning. Imagine the time and the effort that went into it, without the tools we have now.'

I nodded. She didn't need me to talk.

'It's just beyond beautiful.'

'*You* are beyond beautiful,' I stressed, grabbing her hand to pull her around, so she was facing me. 'When you're done, can we take a stroll through the gardens?'

'Yeah, just let me soak it in for a moment more.' She let go of my hand and turned in a circle, breathing it in; absorbing every sight and sound. 'Okay, I'm ready.'

'Let's go.'

THE MOMENT we were at the spot I'd picked out with Jackson and Scarlet, I stopped walking, hoping Atti would follow suit. It was now or never.

Sunshine covered the clearing, the trees slightly blowing with the breeze, creating a peaceful rustling noise.

'Atticus,' I said, using her full name. She raised an eyebrow at me, coming to a halt, crossing her arms across her chest.

'Yeah?' she said, dragging it out. Her scepticism was rife, changing her entire demeanour, which caused a ripple of uneasiness to travel through me. Goosebumps appeared on my arms even though it was a nice, early summer's day.

'You know what day it is?' I asked, hoping she'd give me the answer I wanted. Atticus had always been good with dates—probably something to do with remembering important historical dates—so I felt sure she'd know what today was.

'July 16th?' she said, her voice going up at the end in question.

'Right,' I said, wondering how to egg her on to get where I wanted her to get. Surely she hadn't forgotten?

'And it's the day we became boyfriend and girlfriend when we were sixteen,' she confirmed, smiling, teasing me. Of course she knew.

'You almost gave me a mini heart attack then, A.'

She laughed, throwing her head back, the smile still plastered firmly on her face.

'You shoulda seen the look on your face, P.'

'Oh, ha, ha, funny girl. You got me.'

'Anyway,' she said. 'What were you going to say to me?'

'Right.' I rubbed my hands on my thighs, the nerves reaching a peak. My palms were sweaty; clamming up more and more by the second. 'Atticus.'

I took her hand in mine, hoping she wouldn't notice how hot it was, and held it in front of us. Her shoulder-length brown hair was set in curls that framed her face, a cute ribbon tied in a bow on top of her head, and her eyes were lined with her staple liquid eyeliner. She was beautiful. Every time I looked at her, my breath was taken away. She stole my heart more and more with every moment we spent together.

'Atti, I love you. I've always loved you and these last three months together have been everything I'd hoped they would be and more. Being together as teenagers was perfection, and I didn't think anything could top it. But being together as adults? It's even better than before.'

I squeezed her hand as I fumbled around in my pocket with my other hand. This time, I had a ring she deserved. It was designed specifically for her, and I'd been working on it with the jeweller ever since we bumped into one another at the wrap party. I hadn't known this is how things would go, but I'd been extremely hopeful that they would.

'Every morning and every night, I feel blessed that you are back in my life. That the two of us have got this chance to live the life we always dreamed of. Radley is lucky to have you as his dog mum, and I'm more than lucky to have you by my side. I know you've already guessed this, but I named Radley to remind me of you. You always used to tell me that Boo Radley was misunderstood, with everybody making assumptions about him with no knowledge of the truth. I felt the same way when you wouldn't let me explain about Alexa. You'd made an assumption and seen the worst in me with no reason for it. But like how Jeremy and Scout learned that Boo Radley wasn't the villain they'd believed him to be, I knew that one day you'd realise the same. I just needed to hold out for the day to come. For the stars to align.'

I took a deep breath, the words flowing out of me now, and I couldn't hold them back.

'And damn, Atti. They've aligned.' I laughed a little, as she did the same, rubbing my fingers over hers, the solid feeling of her hand in mine giving me the courage to continue.

Slowly, I peeled my hand out of hers and went down onto one knee, holding out the open ring box in my outstretched hand.

'Atticus,' I said, as the tears filled her eyes. 'I've loved you since we were sixteen, and I love you even more now. Please, do me the honour of becoming my wife. Will you marry me?'

'Yes!' she cried, pulling me up so she could wrap me in the biggest, and tightest, hug.

My heart was full, and I knew that life was about to get very interesting around here.

'YES!' I cried, grabbing him where I could to pull him into a tight hug.

The tears were travelling freely down my face, and I was too overjoyed to even attempt to stop them. I pulled him close to me, and I could feel his heartbeat thrumming away at a fast pace in his chest.

Raising up onto my tiptoes, I grabbed his head in my hands and pulled his lips to mine. The kiss was salty, and soft, and filled with all the love I had for him at that moment.

Parker pulled back from me and took the ring out of the box to place it on my ring finger. The moment I saw it, my heart stopped.

It was one of the most beautiful rings I'd ever seen in my life. The band was platinum with a two-carat marquise diamond placed in the centre with bead-set diamonds on either side. To me, it was perfection. It was vintage looking, yet modern.

'Do you like it? I designed it myself,' Parker said, his worry audible in his tone. 'If you do—'

'Oh, shh you!' I stopped him from saying more. 'I love it, P. Seriously. It's exactly what I would have picked for myself. You just get me.'

'Thank the heavens,' he said with a relieved sigh. Then he took a lungful of air and shouted, 'She said yes!'

A roar erupted from the surrounding trees as our friends and Parker's family swarmed us. With my parents living abroad, I knew they wouldn't be here, but I was so excited to ring them later and let them know. They'd always loved Parker and hoped we would work out our differences.

Congratulations were being said loudly, and I was overwhelmed until Scar came and gave me a big hug.

'I am so happy for you both, Atti,' Scar said, wiping her eyes to get rid of the tears brimming over.

Everybody continued to come from all directions, and I screamed with excitement that there was a photographer who had captured the moment I'd agreed to be Parker's wife.

I'd been so caught up in everything coming from Parker's mouth and actions that I hadn't seen any of them hiding.

The proposal had taken me completely by surprise.

Sure, I'd noticed a couple of sly things he'd done recently—like the time I woke up and he was circling my nana's ring on a piece of paper—and had wondered, but I didn't wake up today knowing I would finish it as Parker Daniels' fiancée. Even when he suggested bringing me to Hampton Court Palace, I didn't bat an eyelid. Just thought it was a nice gesture after everything we'd been through.

Now that I would be though, I couldn't believe it had taken him this long. Parker was impulsive as a rule. I mean, he told me that he loved me the day after we reconnected at the bowling alley. He wasn't one to take things slowly. So the fact he'd taken three months was a long time.

'Let me see the ring!' Cassie called out, rushing towards me from where she'd been hiding in the bushes. Which sounded a lot creepier than it actually was, didn't it? 'Oh, Atti! Do you love it?'

I broke out into a titter, nodding my head as I felt a tear escape the confines of my eye and run down my cheek. It took a lot to make me cry, yet the moment required some emotion. I'd let the boy have that much from me.

'I do!' I gushed, thrusting my hand out so Cassie could admire the large ring on my finger.

A part of me couldn't believe that Parker had designed it for me, because honestly, he'd done such an amazing job. It was the perfect mixture of history and modern taste; completely my style. I loved it and would treasure it for eternity.

'He did amazing!' Cassie beamed, pulling me in for a hug. 'Atti, we're going to finally be sisters!'

'Ahh!' We both jumped up and down, cheering. Growing up, Cassie had always told me that one day we'd be sisters for real, and the fact it was becoming reality made my heart soar. 'How exciting!'

Zara came over next, pulling me into a warm embrace, before letting me go to hand me to Jane.

'Atti, darling!' Her voice soothed me and made my tears pour out a little faster. 'This is the happiest day of my life! You've always been like a daughter to me, and now I get to have you as my daughter-in-law. I feel so blessed. John! John!'

She hollered John's name until he made his way over from

where he'd been congratulating Parker, shaking his hand and giving him one of those father-son hugs that resembled more of an awkward pat down.

'Congratulations, Atti!' he bellowed, pulling me into a real hug, and placing a kiss on my head. 'Happy day! Happy day!'

'Thanks you two,' I said through my tears. 'I am so excited to be a Daniels.'

John let me go, and I faced the two of them, thrilled that Parker had thought to have them here for this.

'Oh, my heart!' Jane touched her chest, her fingers shaking with excitement. 'Atticus Daniels. Oh, it's perfect.'

I smiled from ear to ear, thankful that they wanted me to join their family. I always wondered how it must feel for people who weren't accepted by their in-laws, because it had never been the case for me once. They made me comfortable and happy.

Today, I hadn't just gained a family in Parker and Radley, but I'd gained the entire Daniels clan, too. And with my parents being so far away, and being an only child, I loved that I wouldn't feel so alone.

As they say, the family you make for yourself is the one that truly matters.

'Don't you just love the ring?' Jane asked, grabbing my hand to have a look at it. 'Parker showed me the last time he visited, and it's beautiful. It's the most perfect ring for the most perfect girl for my Parker.'

'I love you both, you know that, right?' I asked them, the tears in their eyes making the ones in mine spill over like an overflowing faucet.

'We love you, sweet girl.'

After I had spoken to everybody, and so had Parker, we

finally made our way back to each other, holding hands tightly, neither of us wanting to let go.

'How did we end up here?' I whispered to him, surveying his family talking with Scar and Jackson, my heart full.

'Fate,' he said simply, as if there was nothing else it could possibly be.

I nodded, agreeing with him.

Drinks were handed out, and Parker gave a toast.

'To Atticus, my future, my life and soon to be wife.'

Everybody cheered, and I took a small sip of the prosecco Scar had handed me. I didn't want to drink too much. I wanted to remember every second of the day.

Scarlet came over to stand beside me, leaning in to whisper in my ear, 'Atti, I need to talk to you.'

'Can it wait?' I asked out of the side of my mouth, eyeing her, not wanting to draw attention to our conversation. I could sense that Scar wanted to tell me something without anybody else hearing.

'I thought it could,' she replied. 'But I need your advice.'

'Okay,' I whispered back. Then, in a louder tone, I said, 'Scar, walk with me to the bathroom.'

The two of us headed off in the direction of the toilet block, and the moment we were far enough away that our voices wouldn't carry back to the group we just left, Scar dropped a bomb on me.

'I slept with Jackson.'

'You what?' I screeched. Scar and I told each other everything, and yeah, maybe she was telling me as soon as she could, but at no point had she even told me she *liked* Jackson in that way. Anytime I asked, she'd fobbed me off, telling me he was just helping her with her acting.

'Don't be too loud!' she hissed, hitting my arm to shut me up. 'Don't make this a big deal.'

'When?' I asked, ignoring her comment about not making this a big deal. She could say what she wanted—this *was* a big deal. Scar hadn't been with a guy in forever, as she'd always said she was putting her career first.

'Errr...' She looked away from me and rubbed her hands together in front of her body. 'Okay,'—she took a deep breath, pushing the air out through her teeth—'so maybe I should have said that I've *been sleeping* with Jackson.'

A gasp left my lips involuntarily. How could she have kept this a secret from me?

'For how long?' I asked, wracking my brain to think of whether I'd noticed a change between them in these last three months. 'Since Parker and I got back together?'

'Maybe a little before that,' she admitted.

'Okay...' I said. 'Well, you've blown me away, I'm not gonna lie.'

'Yeah. Only a handful of times,' she added. 'And when he tries to talk to me about it, I clam up. I don't know what to do. I'm not prepared for a relationship. Atti, I need you to help me.'

I smiled, slightly peeved that she'd taken so long to tell me, but I knew that she'd done what she thought was best for her. Scar's stilted relationship with her parents explained a lot as to why she acted the way she did. That was her story to tell, though.

But there was one thing I knew.

Life was about to get very interesting around here.

ACKNOWLEDGEMENTS

Where do I even start?

To Megan, thank you for always being there for me and helping me through my temper tantrums. You are the main reason I've become an author. I love you.

To Billie, you are one of the best people to have come out of this journey. You keep me going on dark days and you always know what to say. I love you.

To Els, you make me smile and laugh and I live for those times where we get to be just a little bit 'bitchy'. I love you.

To the fam, thanks as always! Growing up in a big family isn't always easy, but I can guarantee you that it's never boring.

To my BETAs, I appreciate you all so much!

To the fourway, thanks for everything. I love you gals.

To every single ARC reader who signed up to give this book a try, thank you, I truly appreciate it.

And thank you, for reading Parker and Atti's story. I hope you stick around for Jackson and Scarlet's.

Thank you all.

ABOUT THE AUTHOR

Katie Lowrie is a twenty-eight-year-old Brit who loves to read and write; basic, right?

A list in no particular order of her greatest loves:

- Henry VIII and the Tudor era
- Her baby cat, Cress
- Musicals
- Disney
- Cheese

She loves to stalk people online (in a good way) and understands if you do too.

instagram.com/klowrieauthor
goodreads.com/klowrieauthor
facebook.com/klowrieauthor
bookbub.com/authors/k-lowrie

ALSO BY K. LOWRIE

Model Act Duet:

Model (mis)Behaviour

Acting Out (Feb 2022)

Printed in Great Britain
by Amazon

69228904R00132